W9-ASI-671

SEP 1986

RECEIVED
OHIO DOMINICAN
COLLEGE LIBRARY
COLUMBUS, OHIO
43219

OHIO DOMINICAN COLLEGE LIBRARY
COLUMBUS, OHIO 43219

JF Ross
Ross, Jane Barks.
The George mediallion

THE GEORGE MEDALLION

Jane Barks Ross

J
R

Copyright 1986 by Jane Barks Ross
All rights reserved
Printed in the United States
ISBN 0-917949-07-2

VIMACH ASSOCIATES

THE PAINTERMAN'S AGREEMENT

The bulky innkeeper stood up, stretched his powerful arms over his head and gave a wide yawn. "Listen to that wind!" he exclaimed to the young man hunched over a long pine table in front of the fire. "I'm glad ye didn't finish the sign today, Alex. This gale would've blown it clean out to Injun country." He shivered in spite of the heat thrown out by the red hot coals banked in the huge fireplace.

The young man, surrounded by a clutter of oil paints and brushes, added a few curlicues to the sign's gold lettering, then held it at arm's length for the innkeeper's approval. "There you are, sir," he said, his voice tinged with a faint burr from the Scottish Highlands. "Is it worth a night's lodgin', Mr. Busby?"

The innkeeper cocked his head and gazed at his new sign with a critical eye. "Aye, lad, it's worth that and more," he replied at length. "Ye've too much talent to waste on signs."

"Not when one likes three meals a day," smiled the artist.

Within the sign's ornate wooden frame was pictured a magnificent stag deer, his golden head held high and arrogantly, his rippling muscles skillfully highlighted in shades of sienna

124677

1

and umber, standing against a background of dark green pine trees. The gold lettering above the noble animal announced that this was the "Golden Stag Inn" — and also that its owner did not want to identify himself too closely with either Tories or Rebels this strange winter of 1792-93.

"Looks like ye can have yer choice of rooms tonight, lad," Innkeeper Busby sighed, his shoulders drooping. "It's not likely we'll have any payin' customers. Only a fool would be travellin' to or from Pittsburgh in this snow. Guess I'll hit the hay."

He had just begun his round of candle-snuffing when the sound of carriage wheels crunching over the frozen road sent both men to the frosted window. Stretching far over the rolling countryside, the snow was a cold blue blanket sparked here and there with patches of ice crystals that flashed and flared with rainbow brilliance. A bitter wind screamed around the eaves of the inn.

"By the heavens above, there's a carriage comin' in the courtyard!" cried the innkeeper. "I'll put more coal on the fire!" He hustled about, preparing for his unexpected guests.

The young artist watched the carriage lurch over the frozen ruts in the road and pull to a halt in the courtyard. In the brilliance of the night he could see it was a very old and a very shabby rig. All the shiny trappings had been removed with the exception of the darkened sidelights, which were green with tarnish. "I doubt if these guests will be verra good at payin' either," he remarked. "Well I'll be gatherin' my paints and be off to bed."

Just then the door flew open and a shrivelled up old man blew in on a furious gust of wind. Fine powdery snow clung to his lashes and a great drop of melting ice glistened at the tip of his red nose. He took a deep breath and scuttled across the room to warm himself in front of the fire.

"A good evenin' to ye, sir," bubbled Innkeeper Busby, beaming upon his guest.

"And how many beds will ye be needin'?"

"Beds shmeds!" retorted the old man rudely. "Who needs beds? It's a hot toddy I'm needin'!" He turned his red-rimmed gaze to the young man gathering his paints. "Yore a limner ain't ye?"

"I am," replied Alex.

"Alexander Keene?"

"The same."

The man gave a sigh of relief. "We've been followin' ye fer days, ever since he," he jerked his head toward the courtyard, "got this bee in his bonnet."

"Followin' me?" Alex frowned in bewilderment. "But why? Who are you?"

"Oh, it's not me that wants ye. Innkeep! A hot buttered rum!" The old man's spirits seemed to rise as his body began to thaw. "It's him out there in the rig who wants ye."

Alex stared. The only person who had ever wanted him had been his mother, and she was long since dead and buried in Edinburgh. He was nothing more than a wandering painter making a meager living by painting new signs for innkeepers who, since the Revolution, no longer wanted their places to be called "The Royal Buck," or "The George Third." Sometimes in the backcountry a portrait of the lady of the house would get him meals and lodging for as long as a week at a time, plus a few coins to jangle in his pocket. But Alexander Keene had been fending for himself for sixteen of his twenty-six years, and nothing the world had to offer surprised him too much. "Well, now, if he wants to see me, why doesn't he come where it's warm?" he inquired.

The little man's eyes shifted to the bug-eyed innkeeper. "Ye'd best go out there," he mumbled.

"You sure you have the right person?" Alex persisted.

"Aye, I'm sure. Get on with it — we've not got all night! Another toddy, Innkeep!" The old man stared greedily at a lump of golden butter melting into the steaming amber grog.

Wrapping a warm knitted scarf around his head, Alex opened the door, braced himself against the icy wind, and made his way through the shadows of the courtyard to the waiting coach. With one hand he tapped softly on the door of the rig; the other he clenched into a big fist. If this turned out to be a trick of some sort, he would be ready. A good fight would warm a body up real good on such a bitter night, he thought cheerfully.

"You may come in, my boy," The educated voice dispelled all hopes for a good brawl. Alex knew from experience that the owners of such voices did not stoop to common brawling. Disappointed, he opened the door and climbed in. Hunched in the far corner of the seat was a man covered by several thick woolen blankets. A tricorn hat was pulled so far down over his face that it almost met the soft beaver collar of his greatcoat. A small charcoal stove at his feet lent the carriage some little warmth. "Close the door," the stranger ordered. "No one must know I am here."

"There must be some mistake, sir," Alex began. "I'm — " he stopped speaking as the man lifted the hat up off his face. In the dimness of the coach it took Alex a few seconds to recognize and assemble the features — the darting hazel eyes, long, prominent nose and sharp, jutting jaw. And when they all blended together into the familiar face from long ago, he gave a sharp cry of surprise. "General!" he exclaimed.

"Aha! You remember!" The man was obviously delighted. "It's been a while since Stony Point. And you were very young. I wasn't sure you'd remember me."

"Sir, I'd not be likely to forget you, now would I?"

The man laughed. "I'm glad to hear it," he said. "I've been trying to catch up with you for days."

"With me? But why, sir?"

The General leaned toward Alex, his eyes burning, and grasped the painterman's bare hands in his own warmly mittened ones. "Because of these!" he cried passionately. "These

hands of yours possess a great talent for painting every detail you see. I have seen every sign you have painted between here and Philadelphia and I am impressed with your ability. And I need it."

Alex was overwhelmed at this praise, but still it did not answer his question. "That's kind of you, sir, but — "

"Do you recall any of the Shawanese language, Alex?" the General countered with a question.

"Oh, a few words, but why?"

"But why am I here in the middle of a nasty winter night? Well, Alexander Keene, I'll tell you why! First, how would you like to strap your painterman's pack on your back and do some commissioned paintings in the western Indian country?"

"The Ohio frontier?" Alex's blue eyes lit up. "Why sir, that would be to my likin', indeed it would. But — "

"But why?" The man began to speak rapidly now. "With your great talent for detail, think what you could paint out there! Landscapes that show the courses of rivers and high points of land strategically right for new forts. Paintings that would show the best places for wide roads to be built through wilderness — roads to lead the Legion of the United States straight into the heart of the Indian power! We must have a chain of American forts from Fort Washington up to the head of the Maumee River. We must end this Indian trouble once and for all in the Northwest!"

Alex mulled all this over in silence.

"There is much talk of carving ten new states out of the Northwest," the man continued. "Sylvania, Michigania, Chersoness, Assenisipia, Metropotamia, Illinois, Washington, Polypotamia and Pelisipia. But the Indians must be — ah — pacified."

"Are the British behind this new trouble?" asked Alex.

"Aha!" The man seemed to catch fire. "There is no doubt the Crown hopes to someday rule America again. In spite of the Treaty of '83, they refuse to surrender their forts at Detroit, Niagara, Oswego and Michilimackinac. They continue to buy the Indians' friendship with many presents — Irish beef, whiskey, flour and handsome silver medallions. Here!" He fumbled underneath the blanket, at last bringing out a small disk that swung from a worn rawhide thong. "One of my men found this on a dead brave."

Alex held the circle of silver to the moonlit window. It was about two inches in diameter, one side showing the profile of George II surrounded by the words: "Georgius Dei Gratia."

"They're not keeping up with the times," grinned Alex. "This shows George II, and George III's been King for some years now!"

"They're all the same to the Indians — their British father," said the General. "These disks were struck a long time ago."

On the reverse side, around the outer rim of the disk Alex made out the words: "Let us look to the most high who blessed our fathers with peace." Toward the center, seated on a rock beneath a tree, a white man offered a peace pipe to an Indian seated on the ground.

"The Indians love them," the man went on. "Well, I'm having silver medallions struck showing President Washington presenting a peace pipe to an Indian! We'll replace King George with George Washington, eh boy?"

Alex shook his head. "And we thought the war was over in '83."

The man's eyes flashed. "The war ended eight years ago in the east. It rages on and on in the west. First President Washington sent General Harmar to destroy the Miami Indian towns, and they defeated him. Then St. Clair took an army up there last November and the Indians slaughtered 'em. St. Clair bungled it all the way." He was talking more to himself than to Alex. "He took an expedition north in October, after the frosts had killed all the grass, and wondered why all his beef-cattle died!" He was silent for a moment, then went on with renewed fire.

"Since St. Clair's defeat, the warriors have come out of the Black Forests of the Northwest yelling the war-whoop past the Moravian ruins on the Tuscawaras, down the Muskingum, Scioto and Miami rivers into Kentucky and Virginia. Why boy, they say it's a sight to curdle your blood! They wear buffalo horns fastened to their heads and are dressed in bearskins, with the scalps of St. Clair's bravest dangling from their belts. They insist the boundary of the United States be the Ohio River instead of the Great Lakes."

"But the Treaty of '83?"

"The only treaty they recognize is the Treaty of Fort Stanwix made over twenty years ago. They say the King had no right to give away lands that did not belong to him in the first place. Then too, there are powerful Americans in the east who prefer the Ohio Country be left a wilderness."

"And why might that be?"

"Selfishness!" snorted the General. "Ben Franklin himself thinks the settlers are outlaw rabble who pick on the poor red man! These men fear new settlements in the west will depopulate the east and reduce their own political power. But these lands are rich and fertile! They were meant to be more than a hunting ground for illiterate savages, or a source of fur for his Britannic Majesty!" He stopped and grinned sheepishly. "There! I've made quite a speech, haven't I?"

"I can see why you were elected to the Congress, sir."

"Ah — yes. Well, truth is I was unseated in the Congress," the General admitted. "I was lucky to get this appointment to train and lead the Legion on this mission."

"General of the Armies! Congratulations, sir!"

"Yes, thank you, Alex. That's why I'm here. The other two failures in the Northwest were due mainly to a lack of information about the enemy's movements. I've already recruited a number of the best woodsmen on the frontier to act as spies.

Now I need some counterspies, along with detailed maps of the Territory. And that's where you come in!"

"Counterspies? You mean, sir, I'm to pretend I'm loyal to the Crown?"

"That's about the gist of it, Alex. Of course, you can refuse to go."

"Not me, sir. I'll go, but I'll not be likin' the company I'll be keepin'."

The man gave his loud, infectious laugh again. "You always wanted to be a portrait painter, Alex. Well, this will give you practice in that too. Paint a portrait of Little Turtle, or Blue Jacket — one of the big chiefs — to send to the British father in London!"

Alex groaned. "You ask a lot, General, askin' a Scot to send presents to the British father."

They both laughed. "How will I be gettin' the paintings to you?" queried Alex.

"You will give them to the man who speaks of the George Medallion and to no one else. He will be the only man alive, except you and me and old Solomon, who will know you are one of our agents."

"The George Medallion?"

"To you and to me, and to your contact, it will mean the George Washington medallion I told you about. To anyone who might overhear it would obviously mean the King George medallion and arouse no suspicion."

"You think of everything, sir." Alex was full of admiration.

"I try to," the General said with attempted modesty. "With enough smart, talented men — like yourself — we'll carve twenty-five fires out of the Northwest Territory before the snow flies next winter!"

"Twenty-five fires?"

"In the beginning we were thirteen colonies, or the thirteen fires as the Indians called us. Now we are fifteen fires — and with the winning of the Northwest we will be ten more fires!

Twenty-five fires! Then perhaps there will be a twenty-sixth and a thirtieth and on and on until this land of ours is a greater power than her Island Mother ever was!" The General would deliver a stirring speech at the drop of a hat, thought Alex. "Did it again, didn't I?" The man read his thoughts and once more they laughed together.

"When do I start, sir?"

"Just as soon as you can find a flatboat going into the Ohio settlements," answered the General. "Go to Simeral's Ferry on the Youghiogheny where families wait for their boats to be built. They are always looking for extra passengers to help defray expenses. And when you find a group that will take you, get word to me by way of my driver, Solomon," He said nodding toward the inn. "We'll be loafing around Simeral's often."

"And when I arrive at the new settlement?"

"Aha!" The General's love of mystery and intrigue was surpassed only by his love of fighting a fierce and cunning enemy. "You will not reach any of the Ohio settlements!"

"Not reach the — "

"It would be too obvious for you to suddlenly appear in their Indian towns, especially in view of all the trouble. You must be taken to the towns!"

"Taken? Do you mean captured?"

"That's the plan."

"What if they decide to take my scalp and leave me?"

"That's up to you. If the George Medallion is spoken of, you will be safe. Another thing — show no surprise at who may be your contact. The identity of some of our agents and spies will surprise you. And if you should be caught, your secret must die with you. The President does not want another Indian war nor another war with the British. Public opinion is against it at the moment. So they will try to negotiate first. But when talking fails — you can't appease an enemy who does not want to be appeased! Anyway, we'll be ready, won't we, Alex?"

"We'll be ready, sir," smiled the painterman.

"And now if you'll send Solomon out — he's probably tipsy by now. And good luck, Alexander Keene. I hope when we meet again it will be on the banks of the Maumee, under the flags of victory!"

When the first bronze streaks of dawn haloed the distant range of mountains, painterman Alexander Keene was still wide awake, staring out of the tiny window of his bedroom.

"Well," he murmured at last, "if that don't take the fat off the 'coon! Old Mad Anthony himself!"

SIMERAL'S FERRY

An early March wind rocked the handful of tents pitched along the banks of the Youghiogheny River. High white clouds raced across the sky, chilling the campers one minute while the unseasonably warm sun melted them the next. Most of the people were busy loading a long, newly finished flatboat anchored at the river's edge, but not twelve-year-old Jubal Hewitt. Jubal was very busy creeping up on a spotted cat sleeping under a budding cottonwood tree near the Hewitt tent. Carefully, silently, he stalked his prey, until he was close enough to swoop the astonished animal up in his arms. With a shout of triumph he turned to the tall sandy-haired young man lounging against an old tree watching.

"I got him, Alex!" cried the boy. "Bring your knife!"

The unhappy cat gave a piteous mew of dispair. It had been caught by this wild youngster before and knew that to resist was to land in the frigid waters of the Youghiogheny.

"You'll be good at stalkin' Indians in the Ohio Country," Alex told the boy,

"D'ya think so?" Jubal's eyes lit up with joy.

"Let's get on with our business, boy," Alex said changing the subject. "That cat's been hidin' from me ever since I lost my best brush crossin' the river. Come on, nice puss, this won't be hurtin' you."

Pulling a wicked looking knife from his deerskin sheath, Alex nodded to Jubal to lay the cat out on the ground . "Hold her tail, lad. Put your finger where the bone ends. All I need is the fine furry tip."

Jubal obeyed, and with a swift flash of the silver blade, Alex relieved the cat of the pointed tip of her tail. A sudden outraged cry made both the man and the boy jump.

"Whatever are you doing to Thankful?" shrieked Jubal's older sister, Polly, dropping a pile of blankets she was toting to the flatboat. "Jubal Hewitt! Mr. Keene! Oh Ma! They're slicin' up Thankful!"

"Oh for Pete's sake, Pol — we're just gettin' a brush for Alex's goose-quill," cried Jubal.

"What kind of man are you, Mr. Alexander Keene?" Polly Hewitt asked, hands on her hips. Her topaz eyes blazed with

anger and her cheeks tinged a deep crimson. "A grown man — abusing a little kitten! And going on the same flatboat with us!"

"But — "

"Oh, shut up, Polly Hewitt!" snapped Jubal. Ever since this painterman had appeared at Simeral's Ferry, sixteen-year-old Polly had been putting on all sorts of airs. Older sisters were a silly lot. "All we wanted was the tip of Thankful's tail for a paintbrush."

"A paintbrush?" Polly stooped to pick up her blankets. Then tossing her chestnut curls, she gave Alex a sidelong glance. "Well, why didn't you say so in the first place?" She huffed down the path to the flatboat, the little white bow of her apron bobbing indignantly from side to side.

"She's painful," muttered Jubal. "Maybe the Injuns'll get her when we get to Columbia." He looked hopefully at his painterman friend for a nod of agreement. But Alex was standing with a silly look on his face, watching Polly's retreating form.

"She's a pretty one when she's mad, isn't she, Jube?" he grinned.

'Ugh!" said the boy. "Let's see you put Thankful's tail in the quill, Alex."

Obligingly the limner slipped the bit of white fur into a sturdy goose quill, swished it over Jubal's sunburned nose and tucked it into his all-weather pack he carried strapped to his back. "Jube!" Alex was suddenly aware of a new burst of activity in the temporary camp. "Your pa's takin' the wheels off the wagons! We're not leavin' for a week, are we?"

"First thing in the morning," replied Jubal. "I thought you knew."

"But why so soon?" Alex seemed alarmed.

"They're afraid if they wait any longer the spring rains will start and flood the Ohio River," the boy told him. "Then it'd be too dangerous to navigate. Besides, the Fosters are real anxious to get started."

When Jonathan Hewitt and his family had arrived from New Jersey the previous fall, they had found the Foster family in a desperate plight. The flatboat they had ordered built was only half finished when poor Increase Foster had run out of money. Upon learning that the Fosters were also bound for the Columbia settlement, Jonathan had offered to pay the balance due if he and his family could travel with them. The Fosters had gratefully accepted, and both families were delighted when, in early February, Alex had appeared with an offer to help defray expenses if they would carry him along. For a full month the three Foster girls and Polly had waged an undeclared war to see who could charm the handsome young artist first.

"But Jube, I can't go yet!" objected Alex.

"And why not, son?" Having heard Alex's comment, Jonathan Hewitt came over and threw a friendly arm around his shoulders.

"Why, sir, I...I was expecting a messenger...with some paints!" stammered the painterman.

"Posh!" said Jonathan. "Plenty of madder roots and burnt earth in the Ohio Country. You can grind your own colors, boy."

Alex gave him a thin smile. He would have to learn to lie better than this or he would surely end up in the middle of an Indian bonfire, or at the wrong end of a British bayonet. But he had to let the General know he was leaving tomorrow. Where in blazes was wizened-up old Solomon? Turning away from the Hewitt tent, Alex wandered to the edge of the dense woods that encircled the camp grounds.

"I don't trust that young man," declared Em Foster in a loud stage whisper after Alex had gone. Em, wife of Increase, was as round as she was tall. She had dimples where elbows should have been and a generous double chin that quivered when she was distressed. And she was often distressed, for she had lost most of her teeth and was unable to eat as much as she would have liked.

"Why not, Em?" Increase tossed a lock of bushy gray hair off his forehead impatiently. "His hair the wrong color?"

"No! Careful of that rocker, Increase! 'Twas my mother's!" snapped Em. "No, 'tisn't the color of his hair. It just don't pay to trust a man that shows all his teeth when he smiles."

Jubal cocked his head. "Reckon if that's true, you're 'bout the only one 'round here we can trust," he blurted out. "Seein' as how you —"

"Jubal! Cut a switch!" roared his father.

"Aw, Pa, I'se just jokin'!"

"You and Miz Hewitt was too old when you had that young 'un," muttered Em Foster, giving Jubal a black look.

"Now, the boy just didn't think before he spoke," Increase Foster's calm voice soothed Em's ruffled feelings.

"He never does!" said Jonathan. "That wagging tongue of his will get him in big trouble some day! Then he'll learn!"

"If we're gonna' leave here in the morning we'd best finish loading." Increase patted Jubal's shoulder, then said in a low tone, "You'd best get out of sight for the nonce." He gave the boy a broad wink.

All that day they loaded the flatboat. The boat was about fifty feet long and twelve feet wide, with low sides of green oak planking. In the bow, stout iron rings had been securely fastened into sturdy posts and would be used to tether the cows, horses and oxen. At the stern, a portion of the boat had been roofed over to make a large, low cabin for living quarters, with a brick hearth at the end for warmth and cooking. Jubal and Inky Foster rolled the heavy wheels slowly down the hill to be stored underneath the wagon bodies. Jonathan and Increase, with the help of the hired boatman, placed the canvas-draped wagons in the bow of the boat. Huge chests filled with a year's supply of linsey-woolsey gowns and men's suits, new leather shoes and hundreds of home-dipped candles were neatly stored inside the covered wagons, safe from the spring rains. Farm implements and furniture were secured in the bow and stern.

"Looks like it might sink, don't it, Jube?" grinned Inky Foster. Ten-year-old Inky had been named after his father, but the confusion caused by having two Increases in the same house was too great, so he had quickly become known as Inky. Like Jubal, he was the youngest of his family, but he was burdened with three older sisters instead of just one. He imitated Jubal in everything, to his mother's disgruntlement.

"She sure does," agreed Jubal. "Come on, Inky, they're startin' the fire for supper. Let's go!"

Dusk was creeping in from the east when the last chest was stored on the flatboat. With the gathering gloom came the damp chill of early spring in the north. The weary men built a roaring fire over which the women hung a kettle of spicy beans and a strip of pork backstrap. The boatmen spitted chunks of pork on sharpened hickory sticks, roasting them over the flames. Jubal sniffed the rich, smoky goodness of the pork fat as it dripped and hissed on the fire. Lying back on a blanket his mother had spread on the cold ground, he watched the shadows from the fire flare and fade from pale to deep blue on the faces of his friends: Em Foster, quiet for once, with her three young daughters, Beth, Sairy and Melissa, beside her; Inky, almost asleep; and the painterman, returned from his moody wanderings, staring into the fire, Polly right beside him. His pa and Mr. Foster were discussing tomorrow's trip with the hired boatmen, while his ma stirred the beans for tomorrow. All around them in the twilight glowed the campfires of other families waiting for their flatboats to be finished. Everything seemed so peaceful and quiet. He wondered whether the new Columbia settlement would be so serene.

A sudden movement in the cottonwood grove caught Jubal's eye. He sat straight up and peered into the gloom. Sure enough! It moved again! Something — or someone — was slinking from tree to tree in the shadowy woods.

"There's someone out there!" he shouted. "Mebbe it's an Injun! Let's go get him!" And with a terrible howl he lit out for the woods.

"SHOVE OFF"

"Jubal!" Alex jumped to his feet and sprinted after the flying form of the boy. The shadow, he thought, might be old Solomon looking for him.

"Ohh," wailed Polly, "they'll be scalped!"

But Jubal Hewitt had no intention of being parted from his thatch of yellow hair. Like a small whirlwind he twisted through the trees, giving sharp, high-pitched barks — his version of the Indian scalp yell. Spotting the shadow directly in front of him, he took a flying leap through the air and caught it around both knees. "Oomph!" grunted the shadow, and fell to the forest floor with a sickening thud.

"I got him! I got him, Alex!" Jubal was wild with excitement. I'll bring the varmint back."

"Carsarn it!" cried the fallen varmint in a very un-Indian voice. "Carsarn it! Ye young divvil — pickin' on an old man like me!"

"Solomon!" cried Alex, hot on Jubal's heels. "I thought it might be you!"

"If ye knowed it was me why didn't ye tie this young dervish down?" Solomon asked bitterly, picking himself up.

"You mean he ain't no Injun?" Jubal's disappointment was keen.

"No, he's just a hungry old man. Come on, old man, there's plenty of food left." Alex led the grumbling driver back to the circle around the campfire.

The men put down their rifles and welcomed the stranger. "Eat well tonight, old timer," said Jubal's father in high spirits. "We won't be here tomorrow night!"

"Eh?" Solomon shot Alex a quick glance. "Shovin' off tomorry, eh? And where be ye bound fer?"

"The Columbia settlement between the Big Miami and the Little Miami Rivers," answered Jonathan. "I built us a house there last year. It's a land of milk and honey — a true garden spot where —"

"—Injuns lurk behind every tree to scalp settlers," Jubal's mother finished the sentence grimly. "Do be still, Jonathan!"

"Now Laura —"

Solomon, his mouth full of beans, gave Laura Hewitt a bleak look. "Ma'am," he gurgled, "if them Injuns are lurkin' behind the trees it won't be to scalp ye. They'll be hidin' from that wild young'un —" nodding toward Jubal.

"Humph!" Em Foster gave Laura a smug I-told-you-so look.

Solomon turned to Increase Foster. "That's quite a pistol ye have there," he said.

Increase's weather-beaten face lit up. "An old gunsmith in Philadelphia made it for me before the Revolution," he explained, handing the gun to the old driver. "It's a snub-nose with brass mounts and a maple stock."

"Pretty fancy carvin' on the handle."

"My initials — I. A. F. Increase Allan Foster!" said Increase with pride. "Wouldn't part with this for a heap of money!"

As they talked the dusk turned to darkness, and soon a thousand blue-white stars sparkled in the clear, cold night sky. Old Solomon, soothed by the good company and food, stood up at last and made his farewells.

"Why not spend the night here?" suggested Laura. "It's so late now."

"Thankee ma'am, gotta get on up the road," said the man. And while the others were busy preparing for the night he turned to Alex and clasped him by the wrist, Indian-fashion. "Good luck, Alexander Keene," he whispered. "I'm off now to report to his nibs." And once again the little man became a shadow slipping silently between the dark tree trunks.

But Em Foster's sharp eyes had caught their parting. "Funny," she murmured to herself. "One would think those two had known each other before."

Everyone was too excited to sleep much that night. Long before the first gray streaks of dawn pencilled across the dark sky, the two families were breaking camp and seeing that everything was safely aboard the flatboat. For there could be no returning — the clumsy boats went one way only, and that way was downstream. After eating a light breakfast and feeding the animals, they said goodbye to the families still waiting for their boats to be finished; then, counting heads, boarded the flatboat. Loud shouts of excitement filled the chill morning air. People gathered along the shore, crying, "Good luck!" and "We'll see you in the summer!" Jubal and Inky Foster hung over the low sides of the boat. Women and girls ran around the deck crying that they would never see the old sod again, while men made doubly sure the animals were securely fastened to their posts.

At long last the big moment arrived! The steersman took his position at the stern of the boat, saw that the six oarsmen and the gouger in the bow were ready, then gave the thrilling cry, "Shove off!" Everyone waved and shouted and one of the boatmen blew a loud blast on his broadhorn. Then, as the awkward craft lurched away from the shore and was caught in the mid-stream current, the voyagers fell silent, watching the oarsmen maneuver skillfully around the boulders and small islands that narrowed this northernmost portion of the river. It was awesome, thought Jubal, being on a private little island in the middle of an ever-widening river, heading into an unknown wilderness.

"I hope we're doing the right thing," Laura Hewitt shivered against her husband's shoulder.

"There's no turning back now, Laura," said Jonathan. "The only home we have is in Columbia."

Soon the golden rays of the rising sun burst from behind the dark chain of mountains, filling the narrow gorge with dazzling light. The trees along the shore were alive with bronze-breasted wild turkeys. Timid deer drank watchfully as

the flatboat bobbled by. Before noon the waters up ahead had changed from a muddy brown to a clear sparkling green.

"That's where the Allegheny flows into the Monongahela to make the Ohio River," explained Jonathan.

"The Ohio River already! I can see Pittsburgh!" shouted Jubal, dangling halfway out of the boat in his eagerness. "What's that dark cloud hangin' over the town, Alex?"

"Smoke, boy," replied the painterman, hanging on to the boy by the seat of his pants. "They burn coal in Pittsburgh — got a lot of the stuff in the hills nearby."

Jubal could make out clusters of log houses, a few frame mansions and numerous brick buildings standing on the triangular plain between the two rivers. Towering sycamores, dusty streets and crowds of milling people; Indians in gay red and yellow blankets with hordes of yapping dogs at their heels; men in stove-pipe hats — all these things were Pittsburgh that bright spring day of 1793.

"You ever been there, Alex?" asked Jubal.

"Once or twice," replied Alex shortly.

"Mr. Keene, why do you want to go into the wilderness and paint Injuns?" Polly turned the full brilliance of her topaz eyes on Alex.

Looking at her, the prospect of painting leather-faced Indians seemed most unattractive to Alex. "Well, Miss Polly," he stammered. "I — well, everyone in the east wants an artist named Stuart to paint their portrait. Now I don't think old Blue Jacket or Little Turtle have ever heard of him, so they'll think I'm pretty good." His eyes twinkled.

Polly laughed prettily. "Oh, Mr. Keene, you're joshing me. Won't it be dangerous?"

"I'm just goin' there to paint, not to enter their fights, Miss Polly." Alex hesitated. "Miss...Polly, if anything should happen to me...well, that is, I will be back...if you'd wait for me..." he blushed to the roots of his hair. "What I mean —"

"We're going to the same place, Mr.Keene," Polly reminded him archly.

Alex took her hand. "What I'm tryin' to say —"

"Ma! Ma! They're lollygaggin'!" Jubal had wearied of hanging over the side of the flatboat looking for hundred pound catfish.

"Jubal Hewitt! I'd like to feed you to the fish!" raged Polly.

Jubal gave his scalp yell and ducked to escape the sting of her open palm on his cheek. "Can't cut a switch here!" he taunted as he scrambled up the side of the cabin.

"Oh, yes, we can!" Jonathan appeared and grabbed his son by his collar. "We're going to tie up for the night pretty soon and unless my eyes deceive me there are plenty of switches waiting to be cut. And you've a backside that's crying to be switched!"

Jubal spent the remainder of the day beside the steersman. Late in the afternoon they tied up on the Virginia shore, for the Ohio River at this northernly point was much too dangerous to navigate after dark. They ate a hot supper of pork stew, then the women and girls went to bed in the cabin of the boat while the men slept around the fire.

The next morning broke chilly and gray, and the little party shoved off in a drizzly rain. The red soil of Virginia stretched out now on the left, the dense forests of the Northwest Territory ahead on the right. After breakfast, Alex gathered all the young people around him at the rail of the boat.

"Pretty soon now you'll see a strip of cleared land. That will be the boundary between Pennsylvania and the Ohio Country."

Jubal stood on tip-toe and squinted through the gray mists. "I see it, Alex," he shouted. "Look, Inky — over there!" The boundary was no more than a wide path cleared of all trees beginning at the river's edge to disappear in the distance.

All at once Jubal shivered. Suddenly he was filled with an overwhelming sense of loneliness. Maybe it was the rising wind that swept across the river, knife-edged with the leftover chill of winter. Or maybe it was the emptiness in his mother's voice as she said, "A path from nowhere leading nowhere." His eyes sought out his painterman friend, hoping for the reassurance of his ever-ready grin, but Alex's face was grim as he stared out into the gray desolation.

Then it came! Low at first, the sound swelled into a terrible, heart-searing scream of human suffering. The blood stopped in Jubal's veins and his temples throbbed wildly. The hired oarsmen froze, their sweeps poised inches above the water. Increase Foster, kneeling at the rail, his bushy gray hair ruffled by the wind, placed one hand over the pistol at his belt. Laura and Polly Hewitt, sitting before the fire in the cabin drying socks, paled. Only Alexander Keene and Jonathan seemed capable of action. "Keep those oars moving!" shouted Jonathan. "We dassent go aground now. Alex, get the rifles! Women, inside the cabin!" His instructions unfroze the others and they obeyed.

"What is it, Alex?" Jubal asked.

"Could be the wind in the trees," replied the limner, hoping against hope this was not his signal to leave the flatboat. If only he had spoken to Polly sooner! "Or a panther."

"Or Injuns?" Jubal asked hopefully.

"Or Indians."

Just then it came again, a long scream of agony. The animals in the bow shuffled restlessly, sensing all was not well. Two of the men on the sweeps knelt down alongside Jonathan and Increase and Alex, their rifles primed and resting on the rail, aimed at the Ohio shore line. As the flatboat wallowed clumsily around the bend of the river, Jubal cried, "What about the other men on the sweeps? Won't they be shot if it is Injuns?"

"They'll have to take their chances," answered his father. "If we should hit a sand bar and it *is* Injuns, we'd all be killed. Don't worry too much, son, the Injuns are poor marksmen."

They all fell silent, hardly breathing at all. It took the boat an eternity to round the curve in the river. And when it had, they all breathed a sigh of relief. For there was no band of painted savages waiting for them around the bend, but one lone man.

"Give aid," he cried piteously when he caught sight of them.

Although the day was gloomy and the shore some little distance away, Jubal saw that the man was white and had a mop of shaggy black hair that failed to conceal a red scar zagging across his forehead. The wind whipped remnants of a torn linsey-woolsey shirt around his broad shoulders. He stood waist high in the water. "Come closer so's I can board. I'm wounded!" he cried.

"Come closer so the Injuns can get our scalps?" answered Jonathan. "You swim out to us."

The man twisted his body, revealing a bloody left shoulder. "I cain't, mister," he moaned. "I jist escaped from the Shaw-

nees — they're after me now! Don't leave me here! They'll kill me awful — " He was screaming again.

Jonathan turned to Increase. "Maybe he's telling the truth," he suggested. "Maybe we should pole in."

"Can't do that, Mr. Hewitt," said one of the sweepsters. "Too many dead logs piled up along the shore. We'd be stuck for sure."

"You don't know how the Shawnees can kill a man," sobbed the man, clutching his wounded shoulder. "Send someone in after me. It's no trick — I swear it by the George Medallion!"

Alex paled. This was it. He gave Polly one last desperate look. "I'll swim ashore and get him," he said. "Maybe he's tellin' the truth and maybe he's not. But none of us would sleep tonight if we didn't know for sure." And plunging into the tumbling water, he began to swim to shore.

The people on the flatboat watched in numb silence, the men kneeling on the deck, the women and girls peeking around the sides of the cabin. Jubal had a fleeting impulse to follow his idol; only the fact that he could not swim kept him on the boat.

With smooth, powerful strokes the painterman neared the Indian side until at last he reached the quagmire of half-sunken old logs and rotting tree limbs. He pulled himself up over the tangled debris and onto the pebbled beach where the white man awaited him. Immediately the air was filled with terrible yells as seven or eight garishly painted savages leapt from the underbrush. Jubal saw a fat Indian brave grab Alex around his chest and pull him out of sight. He glanced quickly up at Polly. Her face was a white mask of horror. "Don't worry, Pol," he quavered, "Alex'll get away — " But his knees were shaking and in his heart he felt none of them would ever see the merry painterman again.

"Keep her in the channel, boys," shouted Jonathan. "Keep her on a true course or we're all done for!"

The men fired several volleys of shot at the shore, but strangely enough there was no answering round from the guns of the red men. As suddenly as they had appeared, they were gone, and so was the white man. The wind moaned through the trees on the lonely shore and spat gusts of cold rain against the flatboat. The lazy river flowed along as if nothing had happened.

"Oh, someone go and get him!" cried Polly, coming to life.

"Polly girl, we can't do that — they'd just kill whoever went," said Jonathan.

"But we just can't go on and leave him there to die!" sobbed the girl.

"Polly," her father said gently, "he's either alive and a prisoner on his way north, or he's — he's already dead. In either case, there's nothing we can do."

"Oh!" Polly buried her face in her mother's lap.

That night they found a small cluster of cabins sprawled along the Virginia shore, and there they tied up for the night. No one was hungry. No one was sleepy. They were all quiet, each lost in thought about this new Ohio Country. Jubal sat in despair watching the flames turn the flatboat a rosy pink. Polly had gone to bed to cry herself to sleep. An air of gloom hung over the new settlers.

"It's not the same without him," Laura Hewitt wiped a tear from her eye.

"Imagine a white man doing that to his own people!" said Melissa Foster. "The renegade!"

Jonathan shook his head. Had he been wrong to bring his family into this savage new land? "It could have been any one of us," he remarked.

Em Foster, who had been still since Alex's capture, rubbed her forehead. "It could have been," she began slowly, "until that renegade said 'I swear it by the George Medallion'."

They all stared dumbfounded at the plump woman. "What are you getting at, Em?" asked Increase.

"Well, I'm not sure myself — but all the time that man was moanin' there on the shore that painterman just stood, kinda' like he was waitin' for something. Then when he heard those words, he got white as milk and jumped overboard."

"So the man had a decent and brave impulse," Laura Hewitt spoke impatiently. "You never did like him, Em."

"No, I didn't," Em admitted. "But there's more to that young man than meets the eye."

"Showed all his teeth when he smiled," Increase teased her.

Em ignored him. "Why didn't the Injuns fire back at us?" she demanded.

"Oh, Ma," cried Beth, "you're always imagining things."

"Well then, Miss Smarty, tell me what a George Medallion is!"

"Why — I don't know," replied Beth. "What is it?"

"It's a silver medallion the British present to the Indians to keep them friendly to the Crown," Jonathan explained.

"Well, then," Em warmed to her subject. "There you are!"

They looked at one another dazedly. "You mean, Em, you think Alex was — is a British agent?"

"A British spy!" burst out Em. "What else? Remember that old man back at Simeral's that Jubal almost killed? You mark my words, Alex knew that man!"

"No!" Jubal jumped to his feet in sudden anger. "No! Alex couldn't be a British spy!"

"Jube! Go to bed," ordered his father.

"She shouldn't say that about Alex," Jubal's eyes flashed. "Him bein' captured only this mornin'!"

"Did he say anything that night in the woods, son?" asked Jonathan.

"Nothin' — he said nothin'!" answered Jubal hotly.

"Are you sure?"

"He said —" Jubal stopped short, remembering. "He said, 'Solomon, I thought it might be you'."

"I knew it! I knew it!" said Em.

"Oh!" Jubal gave a strangled cry. "I still don't believe he's a spy!" And he ran blindly down the river bank to the flat-boat. He'd never, never believe his painterman friend was in the pay of the British. And neither would Polly!

COLUMBIA!

The next morning the steersman issued firm orders. "From now on, no one goes ashore — for any reason! Not 'till we reach Columbia!"

To the relief of the new settlers on the flatboat, the remainder of the trip was uneventful. And as the bright spring weather returned, their gloom lifted. After they passed Fort Henry at Wheeling they were able to travel day and night, for there the river straightened out and the channel broadened. One day in late March a storm whipped up the great river until its surface was foamy white.

"They should have named it the White River," Jubal remarked to his father as they huddled close to the fire trying to keep warm and dry.

"They did, son," replied Jonathan.

"They did? I thought it was the Ohio," giggled Jubal.

"The Miami word 'O'hui,' or 'Ohi,' means 'very white'," his father explained. "And 'Ohi opeedhanne' means 'white foaming river.' So you see, it really is the White River."

After the lashing storm that rocked the boat sickeningly from side to side, the weather turned cold again and the people spent most of their time warming themselves at the fire.

The men took turns keeping watch for Indian attacks. Whenever they approached a settlement the steersman blew long, eerie-sounding blasts on his broadhorn to announce their impending arrival. It made Jubal's blood run cold to hear the weird music echo from hill to hill in the lonely wilderness. But it meant they were nearing a town where excited people lined themselves along the shore to wave to the newcomers. Slowly they drifted past the mouth of the Little Muskingum, past Duck Island with its giant mottled sycamores. They glided by Fort Harmar and Marietta, Kanawha and the Frenchie's town of Gallipolis. And as the gales of March brought the first soft rains of April, great patches of white appeared on the hills that rose steeply on either side of the river.

"Looks like winter," shivered Melissa Foster. "That's dogwood, M'lissa. Dogwood winter," her mother told her.

Polly was still shocked by the violence that had come to Alex. The mere sight of Thankful waving her stubbly tail was enough to reduce the girl to tears. She sat in the cabin, listless and disinterested. Jubal tried to cheer her up. "Don't believe what they're sayin' about Alex, Pol," he said. "Alex isn't a spy. He just wanted to paint Injuns — and Pol, if he is alive, he'll find his way back to Columbia."

Polly raised her topaz eyes to look at him and Jubal winced at the deep purple shadows under them. "Remember what he said, Pol, about waitin' for him?" he asked encouragingly.

"He might have said more if you hadn't been such a bigmouth!" Polly's old spirit flashed briefly.

Jubal hung his head. "Yeh, I know, Polly. I'm sorry. I just didn't think."

"You never think — that's your trouble!" snapped Polly. "Oh, Jube, I'm so sick of this never-ending wilderness. I want to go back home." A tear rolled down her pale face.

They were interrupted by the lusty clamor of the broadhorn. "We're there! We're there!" Inky Foster rushed into the cabin. "Come on out, Jube — there's a big crowd waitin' for us! It's Columbia!"

Jubal gave an excited yell and dashed out onto the deck with Inky. Both boys threw their feet over the side of the flat-boat and sat on the narrow rail, shouting for the boatmen to hurry and pole them ashore. And when the boat scrunched the sandy bottom, they jumped off and scrambled up the bank to explore their new home.

Columbia looked beautiful to Jubal that bright April morning. The town was made up of fifty or more log houses scattered on a flat, sun-dappled plain. A small stockade stood off to one side and several blockhouses had been built at intervals along the river. Dozens of tree stumps cluttered the fields, and at the edge of the clearing loomed the brooding forests.

The grown-ups left the boat amid a great deal of confusion. Tearful reunions with old friends from the east blended with joyful welcomes from new acquaintances, all happy to have the new settlers among them. As soon as he could, Jonathan Hewitt led his wife and two children straight back from the beach to the foot of a sugarloaf hill, where a small hewed log house stood. Its narrow door of thick oak planks turned on stout wooden hinges. Above the door Jubal noticed tiny portholes just large enough to rest the barrel of a rifle. Two small windows, each set with four panes of glass, were placed high on either side of the door. Inside was a huge stone fireplace, one built-in bed, a rough oak table and several chairs.

"Jubal, gather some wood for a fire," Jonathan ordered. "Laura, make yourself comfortable — I'll go start unloading." And without so much as a glance at his wife, he was gone.

"Land of milk and honey my eye!" Laura swatted at a pesky mosquito. "Land of many bugs if you ask me!"

"Well," Polly brushed a cobweb from her face. "I'll fetch a broom and the ticks — at least we can sleep warm tonight!"

It was a busy afternoon. The men led the animals off the flatboat and unloaded chests and farm implements until dark. The women scrubbed and swept until the wood floors shone white and the stone hearth gleamed. They scoured windows, brushed cobwebs from the corners, and laid huge cherry logs in the fireplace. At supper time, helpful neighbors appeared from across the fields bringing kettles of spicy venison stew and pitchers of sweet milk to the newcomers. After supper the Hewitts sauntered across the broad plain to say goodnight to the Fosters, whose cabin stood close to the river.

Before long the cricket-song filled the spring twilight and the Hewitts went back to their own cabin. Jubal and Polly sat with their parents before a blazing fire in the deep fireplace and talked until their eyelids drooped. Then, after prayers of thanks for their safe arrival, they fell onto their down ticks and were asleep in no time.

Polly never knew what wakened her in the small hours of the morning. Perhaps it was the damp chill that crept through the house as the fire burned low. Or perhaps it was the quick padding of squirrels feet as they darted across the clapboard roof. She shivered and got up to put another log on the fire, glancing at the tick on the floor where Jubal was sleeping until they could get the loft ready.

Her heart jumped to her throat. There was no one there! Swiftly she glanced about the dim room. No Jubal. She knew he could not be up in the loft because as yet there was no ladder. "Ma! Pa!" she screamed, "Jubal's gone! Oh, the Injuns got him already!"

Jonathan Hewitt sat bolt upright and blinked. "Jubal?" he mumbled sleepily. "Where'd he go?"

"I don't know! The Injuns took him — Pa! Wake up!" Polly was frantic.

Laura woke with a start and sprang up to put both arms around her distraught daughter. "Polly, dear, you're having a nightmare, poor baby," she soothed. "What was it about — Alex?"

"Oh, Ma, it's Jubal! He's gone," sobbed the girl. "First Alex, now Jube. Oh, why did we ever come to this awful place?"

A thorough search of the cabin proved her right. Jubal was nowhere to be found. Jonathan, fully awake now, grabbed his rifle and said, "Stay here, you two. I'll look outside. And don't open the door for anyone but me!" He paused to examine the latch string. "Looks like it's been opened from the inside."

"That's it!" cried Polly, "An Injun crawled in through the window and stole him!"

"For heaven's sake, girl, use your head! No Injun over two years old could fit through those tiny windows," snapped Jonathan. "Besides, the glass isn't broken." He let himself out into the moonlit night.

There was no sign of the boy. Columbia lay sleeping under a starry sky, peaceful and serene. The moonlight made a silver path across the tranquil river. Jonathan fired his gun several times, calling his son's name after each discharge. Only the hungry wolves from the nearby forest replied.

"Those beasts have eaten him! Oh, p-poor J-Jubal," stammered Laura, as alarmed by now as Polly. Both women had ignored Jonathan's strict orders to remain inside and stood close behind him barefoot and in bedgowns, their teeth chattering with cold and worry.

Some of the neighbors, hearing shots, came running across the plain. "What's wrong?" hollered Sam Kibbey. "Injuns steal yer horses?"

"My boy's missing," replied Jonathan tersely. "Polly, take your mother inside. Mr. Kibbey and I will search the woods. He can't be too far away."

"You go to the river, I'll search the woods, I know 'em better'n you do!," suggested Sam.

The river! Jonathan felt his mouth go dry. He raced off toward the beach without another word.

In her cabin at the river's edge, Em Foster dozed fitfully. She was cold. She had sent Increase to the flatboat for a chest of blankets he had forgotten to bring in earlier. She flounced her plump self over on her feather tick — then her eyes flew open wide. What was that noise? Someone or something was sneaking up on her house! Em held her breath. Sure enough, there it was again: a faint rustling in the tall grass. Probably a bear. Or — her flesh crawled — Indians. Her eyes darted up toward the loft where her three daughters and Inky were asleep then back to the thick oak door — she let out a muffled cry of despair. Increase had forgotten to take in the latchstring! Anyone, bear or Indian, could enter at will and murder her before any of her family knew she was even in danger!

Now, thanks to Increase's carelessness, she must tip-toe over to the door and bar it at once. As for Increase out there in the darkness, well, he must take his own chances with the dangerous prowler. She wished him well. Em had one bare foot out on the wood floor when she heard someone fumbling with the latchstring. She sat rigidly on the edge of her bed, watching with horrified fascination as the door began to swing back. She opened her mouth to scream but no sound came. Wider and wider opened the door, until it revealed not the painted savage she expected, but a small, white clad ghost. In the blue-white light of the moon its' image was terrifying. It came toward her with both arms outstretched.

Em Foster pulled in one quivering breath, which restored her power of speech. "It's a ha'nt! It's a ha'nt!" she screeched, and plunged wildly past the wraith into the frosty night giving a series of panicky squeals that sent goose bumps up the spine of everyone in the settlement.

Awakened by their mother's shrieks, the three Foster girls and Inky thrust their heads down from the loft. Sairy, the first on the ladder, was the first to see the white clad figure standing in the middle of the shadowy room. "A ghost!" she screamed. "Oh, help!"

At her sharp cry the ghost dropped its arms and opened its eyes. "Where am I?" it asked blinking in confusion.

Sairy Foster clung to the ladder, her eyes bulging. "You... you're not a ghost..you're Jubal Hewitt!" she gasped. "You're walkin' in your sleep! Oh! You look so silly!" And she burst out laughing. Beth and Melissa, right behind her, stared for a moment then threw back their heads and shouted in merriment. Loyal Inky came to his friend's defense. "Wake up, Jube," he urged.

Jubal rubbed his eyes. "How'd I get here?" he mumbled.

"You walked in your sleep, that's how," replied Inky. The three girls had dissolved into helpless giggles.

"Oh, oh," cried Sairy, holding her sides, "if he can scare Injuns like he scared Ma — we've nothing to worry about!"

"He's shiverin'," Inky pointed out. "Give him a blanket, Sairy, and stop gigglin' or I'll tell about the time you —"

"Inky!" warned Sairy, sobering.

Poor Jubal! That he was chilled to the bone was bad enough, but the embarrassment was worse. To be caught in his sleeping gown in a covey of silly girls! And if he could judge by his own sister, they would have the news all over the settlement by sun-up.

Just then his father, followed by Increase and the babbling Em, dashed into the room. "Jubal! What the blazes are you doing here?" demanded Jonathan, his tone a mixture of irritation and relief.

"Oh!" moaned Em, "I should've known that dreadful boy was the cause of all this!"

"Now, Em, he didn't do it apurpose," Increased soothed her. "There's been too much excitement today for a boy. Been too much for me," he grinned sheepishly. "I fell asleep on the boat."

Em gave a snort and waddled back to her bed. Jubal's father wrapped a blanket around his unhappy son and they headed for their own cabin. "Come on, boy, your Ma and Polly are crazy with worry," he said. "We'll bring your blanket back tomorrow, Increase."

"I have a feelin' about that boy," muttered Em when they had gone. "He's likely to be the death of me yet!"

After that burst of excitement the community settled down to everyday living. The Hewitts planted a small patch of corn for roasting, along with pumpkins, squash, beans and potatoes. Laura lovingly placed her pewter plates and mugs on the mantel in an attempt to make the one room cabin something like their home in the east. Polly made friends with the other young people and tried to put the painterman out of her thoughts. Thankful's tail was beginning to sprout a fine new tip, even more pointed than the one she had lost. "He was only a British spy anyhow," Polly said scornfully to Jubal, her eyes too bright.

Jubal stiffened. "You don't *know* that, Pol," he objected. "You're just takin' that gossipy Em Foster's word for it."

Polly sighed. "Well, she's probably right."

Before sunrise every fair morning the men and boys started out for Turkey Bottom to tend the corn fields. About a mile and a half east of Columbia, Turkey Bottom was a rich plain marked off into lots of five acres each, which were owned by individual settlers. The whole acreage was enclosed by a high stockade fence. Jubal loved the walk through the woods to the Bottom. Above the song of the redbird he could sometimes hear the rumbling drum of the partridge, or the plaintive wail of the dove, or the loud gobble of the wild turkey. Once in a while a timid deer, aroused from its thicket bounded gracefully off, clearing logs and bushes with a single leap. Wild herbs lent their spicy fragrance to the balmy air and the ground was covered with mayapple, bloodroot, ginseng and delicate lavender violets. The excitement of just being alive almost overcame Jubal on these walks. When they reached the Bottom he drove the oxen while his father, followed by the corn dressers, guided the plow between the rows of corn. The white men tilled the ancient fields of the red man with their firearms beside them. Sam Kibbey had three horses stolen by renegade Indians, and no one knew when — or if — an attack would come.

On rainy days when there was little or no wind, Jonathan took his son hunting in the deep forests that stretched unendingly toward the north. On such days the deer kept to the open woods on the highest ground they could find. Sundays the whole family went to the little church on the knoll and listened to white-haired old Reverend Gano deliver the Gospel in his tremulous voice.

Once Jubal went with his father and Ian Campbell to the floating mill on the Little Miami to grind corn. Built in an old flatboat, its wheel turning slowly with the natural current running between the boat and a small dugout anchored in the stream, the mill had only one pair of small stones, so only a small amount of meal could be ground in a single day.

As the spring days lengthened and twilight lingered over the river, the people of Columbia were more hopeful than ever before. The east had finally recognized the frontier's need for protection and had sent General Anthony Wayne to Fort Washington to train the troops against the Indians. He had stopped briefly at Columbia on his way to Cincinnati, but Jubal had been at the Bottom and had missed seeing the great man.

"Shucks! I wish I'd seen him," said Jubal to his father.

"You're going to get a chance to see him, Jube," answered Jonathan. "You've been a big help to me this summer," the man wiped his forehead. He was more used to scolding his bright-eyed son than to praising him. "Ah — how'd you like to visit Fort Washington over the Fourth of July?"

FORT WASHINGTON

Jubal's heart almost flew out of his mouth at his father's words. Fort Washington — the great city of Cincinnati on the Fourth of July! "Ya hoo!" he shouted, "You and Ma goin' too?"

"No, there's too much work to be done," replied Jonathan. "Some officers from the fort are coming to pick up the Foster girls and Polly, so your ma and I figured you and Inky might as well go along. Em Foster's going to chaperone —"

Jubal flushed at the mention of the Foster girls. Every time they caught sight of him they burst out laughing. "Shucks!" he murmured.

"Don't you want to go?"

"Oh sure, 'cept those gaggy Foster girls —"

"They'll forget it after a while," his father assured him. "You'll be surprised at what those girls will forget when they see handsome young soldiers! And Jube, poor Em Foster is sure you've put a curse on her, so be a good lad and try not to frighten the poor soul again." He placed a friendly arm around his son's shoulder and hid a smile.

"Shucks!" repeated Jubal, kicking the blossom off a bluebell.

The morning of July third dawned hot and clear. It would be a magnificent day for a boat trip, thought Jubal excitedly. He dressed in a summer roundabout and pantaloons with mould buttons and a blue double-breasted silk vest with two rows of small plated sugarloaf buttons. Polly, he thought, had never looked prettier. Her chestnut hair combed up in back, fell in loose curls over her forehead and her amber-colored eyes shone in her suntanned face. Her dress of the palest green was fashioned with a low ruffled neck and a full skirt that fell in soft folds from a high-waisted yellow sash. Her flat heeled shoes were richly embroidered and a yellow parasol sheltered her face from the sun. It was good to see Polly happy again.

"Look at Mrs. Foster," whispered Jubal to his sister as they neared the Foster cabin where they were to meet the barge that would carry them downriver. "I don't see how she can walk 'thall those skirts on."

Em Foster was resplendent in her Sunday best. It was not every day one chaperoned a party to the city! Her face, shiny from the heat, was almost hidden by a bonnet that tied under her chins with lavender ribbons. In spite of the heat, she wore many quilted petticoats under her gown of pale blue silk. She winced when she saw Jubal, but the peaceful beauty of the mid-summer day allayed her misgivings.

Eight young officers from the fort were waiting in the barge at the river's edge. Tall, young and sun-bronzed, the officers were smartly dressed in dark blue cutaway coats faced with bright red, snowy white vests and leggings, and stiff white belts. Their round hats were trimmed with roaches of bearskin and cloth bands with cockades and feathers. The morning sun sparkled brilliant white-gold stars on their highly polished brass buttons and glinted on the slim swords that swung at their sides. There was much gay chatter and a great deal of eyelash fluttering as the girls boarded the barge and met their escorts.

"Silly, ain't they?" muttered Inky to Jubal as they trailed behind.

"Silly!" Jubal agreed heartily. But his Pa had been right. As long as the girls were flirting with the officers they were not teasing him. "Bye Pa! Ma!" he shouted as the barge left shore. "See you in a week!"

Jubal was mistaken. One year would pass before he saw any of his family again.

The hour long trip to Cincinnati passed too quickly. A soft summer breeze fanned across the wide river, swaying the cottonwoods and the willows along the shore. Golden sunlight glittered on the ripples sent out by the dipping oars. Not far from the pebbled beach Jubal could make out the narrow road that led from the city to Columbia. All to soon they swept around a bend in the river, and there it stood — Cincinnati! Fort Washington, at the east end of the city, gleamed with new coats of red paint. The long, low buildings stretching along the river were bright with flags and bunting, and crowds of excited people perched on the hills to watch the barges bring holiday vistors ashore.

The officers showed their guests where they were to stay during their visit. In high spirits, the girls left their valises in the log guest house and frolicked off with the young men for a sight-seeing jaunt through the fort and the city. Jubal and Inky took off on their own while Em, panting and warm, decided to rest from the arduous trip.

On the morning of the Fourth, Jubal was awakened by the deep-throated 'VROOM!' of the fort's cannon. Thirteen rounds came from its mighty innards. Twelve more issued forth at noon, followed by a display of troops marching under arms. It was a thrilling sight! One sub-legion followed another, dressed in their handsome navy and white dress uniforms, one unit with red cockades on their hats, another with bright green — Jubal decided then and there he must become a soldier when he grew up!

"Which one is General Wayne?" he asked Polly's escort.

"Wayne? Oh, he left here in May," the man told him. "Said Cincinnati was too wicked a place for his soldiers. Went to a place called Hobson's Choice farther west."

"Shucks!" This was the second time Jubal had just missed seeing the great man.

But he could not remain disappointed long amidst the gaiety of Fort Washington. Sunlight filtered through the towering trees, dappling the dusty ground. Young girls dressed in their best gowns looked like colorful splashes of soft blue and emerald, turquoise and old rose as they rustled from group to group. The deep rumble of men's voices and the tinkling laughter of the girls mingled with the shouts of children and the sharp yipes of excited dogs. For Jubal and Inky it all blended together to make the most exciting day of their young lives. And the best was yet to come!

After a gala dinner and more artillery fire, after darkness had fallen over the frontier fortress — then came the fireworks! The two boys sat on the river bank and gasped at each burst of dazzling brilliance that rained down from the night sky to be reflected in the glassy waters of the black river.

"We get t'see them twice, Jube," commented Inky. "Once in the sky and again in the river."

And then came the grand ball for the grown-ups. "Let's stay up and watch 'em lollygag," suggested Jubal.

"I'm sleepy, Jube," protested the younger boy. "Besides, I don't feel so good."

"Posh!" sniffed Jubal. "It only comes once a year. You can stand it. Come on!"

The boys spent two more days prowling the nooks and crannies of the fort until poor Inky almost wept from weariness and a stomach ache. "Jube, I'm sick," he croaked. "Let's find Ma and go home!"

"Oh, Inky — all right!" Jubal did not want to admit that he too was a little tired of the hustle and bustle and noise of the

place. He sat Inky under a tree and went in search of Em.

Em Foster took one look at her son's flushed face and put a hand over his forehead. "I reckon I'd best get him home," she said. "Jubal, run down to the river and see if there's a canoe goin' up river this afternoon. I'll tell the girls. They may as well stay their full week — mebbe they can find themselves husbands if they stay a little longer." She waddled off, talking to herself.

"Can I go too, Mrs. Foster?" queried Jubal. "I'm ready to go home too."

Em gave him a tortured look. "I...I guess so," she said reluctantly.

The canoe Jubal found already had one passenger, and he had obviously celebrated too much. He gazed owlishly at the two boys and the plump woman. "Hic," he said gravely.

"Don't mind him, ma'am" said the polesman. "Jes' get in, you and the littlest boy."

Em paused. "Why not both boys?" she demanded.

The man swallowed and stared up at the cloudless sky. "Welllll," he hesitated. His reasoning became clear to Jubal as Em lowered her generous bulk gingerly into the middle of the canoe. Instantly the waterline crept dangerously near the top edge of the craft. The man held his breath and wondered if he should give the call to abandon ship. "Now," he said when the crisis was past, "put the sick boy in the stern and you — " he nodded toward Jubal — "you walk along the road. We'll keep you in sight. And don't try to talk to us — you might attract Injuns."

Before starting out on the dusty road Jubal took off his shoes and tossed them into the canoe. He could not stand to wear the tight, hot things another minute. The warm earth felt good to his aching feet. Now and then he stopped to send small, flat stones skimming over the surface of the river. The canoe slid silently through the water beside him, hugging the shore as closely as it dared. The green forest on his left was bright with shafts of golden sunlight. Swarms of tiny gnats hung lazily on the still air. Jubal thought his heart would burst with happiness. He was so glad to be returning to the cabin by the sugarloaf. He had so much to tell Ma and Pa — maybe next Fourth of July they could all go to the city! Forgetting the polesman's warning, he broke out into a lusty chorus of a song Alex had taught him back at Simeral's. "Ohh, the Blue — Bells — of Scotland — "

Suddenly the owlish-looking man in the canoe came to life. He lurched foreward, clutched both sides of the boat and cried out, "She's too fat! She'll sink us!" And with great dignity he stood up, put one long leg straight out in front of him and stepped out of the canoe into the water. The flimsy canoe wobbled once then turned over, throwing its startled occupants head first into the river.

"Oh, help! Oh, I'll drown — Inky, where are you?" shrieked Em Foster, flailing her hands in the water.

"You're all right, ma'am," sputtered the polesman through a mouthful of water. "It's shallow where you are — just wade in!"

Inky was clinging to the upset canoe being carried downriver by the current. "You can touch bottom, Ma!" he yelled. "Wade in!"

For a brief instant Jubal stood rooted to the ground. Then he dashed to the river and waded as far out as he could, both hands outstretched. "Kick the canoe in here, Inky," he called. "In here, Mrs. Foster — I'm here —"

The sharp crack of rifle-fire stopped him short. One shot, then another — and yet a third! Why would anyone be shooting at drowning people? Jubal wondered, turning to peer up at the river bank. Then his blood ran cold. Through a white cloud of gunsmoke he glimpsed the blackened faces of two Indians. Yelling fearfully, they ran down the embankment and plunged out into the shallow water toward him, the largest of the two holding a tomahawk in one hand and a scalping knife in the other.

Desperately Jubal looked for someplace to retreat. There was only the river — and he could not swim. He was trapped! He made one blind dash to the right, but it was futile. One Indian seized him around the shoulders, while the other extended a hand in a gesture of peace. Jubal knew that, for the moment, his life would be spared.

Before the braves pulled him up the hill toward the north, he cast one last anguished look at the river where his friends were thrashing for their lives. The drunken man was floating on his back. The polesman had caught up with Inky and was kicking them both to the opposite shore. But strangest of all was Em Foster. Em, her many quilted petticoats spread out over the water and her head near the surface, was floating gently on the current back to Fort Washington, howling at the top of her lungs.

"It's that dreadful boy!" she wailed, "I knew he'd be the death of me — Oh! Help!"

Jubal gave a piercing cry. "Tell 'em the Injuns got me," he screamed. "Tell Pa and Ma —"

He wondered if they heard him at all. They were all so preoccupied with saving their own skins. Then his captors jerked him along with them until he soon lost sight of the river.

TO THE NORTH!

The two Indians started off at a dogtrot, dragging the unhappy Jubal between them. Up steep slopes, down into rugged valleys they jogged. Whenever they waded through a stream and out again, the smallest Indian motioned for Jubal to step in his tracks while his companion followed, treading over both tracks. Jubal's spirits sank at this, for he knew it would be impossible for anyone from the fort to follow and rescue him. His brain worked feverishly to plot some way of escape. Finally at sunset they halted on a low point of dense woods near a rushing, amber colored brook.

The smaller of the two red men pointed to himself. "Wawpawmawquaw," he said. "Me White Loon. Him Nawakwa." He pointed to his friend. And without another word he began kindling a fire while Nawakwa went in search of game. Before long the hunter returned with a fat raccoon, which he proceeded to dress by burning off the hair and cutting it into hunks to be broiled over the fire. Jubal studied his two captors as he gulped the crispy meat. White Loon, dressed in a breechcloth and moccasins, was a little over middle size and well formed. His face had sharp features under the black war-paint, and he seemed much younger and more agreeable than his surly partner.

"I'm Jubal Hewitt," said Jubal cheerfully. Maybe — just maybe — if they thought he did not mind going with them, they would let him go. "I'm sure glad to be gettin' away from my family! My Pa beats me something awful." He glanced quickly at the two Indians. Their faces were impassive. "Yep! Beats me bloody every night. And my Ma — you oughta see how she starves me!" Jubal was beginning to enjoy the lies he was telling. "The others don't like me much either. Old Em Foster says I'm a jinx. Say —" he stopped suddenly. "Maybe you two don't talk English, huh?"

The White Loon shook his head. "No Inglish," he grunted.

"And him?"

"No Inglish."

"Well, why didn't you say so before, you greasy old skunk?" snorted Jubal. "And you — " he turned to Nawakwa, "you're about the ugliest critter I ever did see!"

"Onee," replied the Ugly One politely.

After the meal the two Indians looped the middle of a cord around Jubal's neck, extending around his wrists separately, then spread a dirty blanket on the ground and ordered him to lie down. Stretching themselves on either side of the boy, they passed the ends of the cord under their bodies and covered themselves with the remaining blanket.

Jubal lay awake long after his captors had fallen asleep. Great waves of regret swept over him as he stared up into the velvety night. If only he had heeded the polesman's warning and kept quiet the Injuns probably would not have spotted them. He might have gotten them all killed! Maybe Polly was right — maybe he did not think before he spoke or acted. Maybe one of those stars twinkling in the heavens was his own ill-fated star. He hoped desperately that Inky and Em Foster and the polesman and even the drunk had reached shore safely. He hoped someone would tell his pa what had happened, and he swore by all the stars in the heavens that if he ever escaped from this predicament he would be more careful in what he said and did! A single tear of self-pity rolled down his cheek, then before he knew it, he too was asleep.

The Indians were up before daybreak. Untying Jubal, they ate the remains of the raccoon. After examining the priming of their rifles, they shouldered their baggage of two blankets, a bridle, a cord and — Jubal shuddered — a scalp. White Loon carried a deerskin-wrapped object he seemed to prize very highly. And before the sun was more than an orange glow in the eastern sky they were on their way, marching single file due north. It was going to be a glorious day. The sky was clear and the air balmy; the country, now less hilly, was covered with soft green moss and gay wild flowers. To Jubal's relief they walked today instead of jogging.

About noontime they came to a large opening where the Indians moved cautiously, half bent with their rifles trailing. A little farther on they stopped in a deep ravine and White Loon, taking a bridle, vanished silently into the hollow. A short time later he returned, mounted on a handsome cream-colored horse he had apparently just stolen. That night they camped in a low, rich bottom near a crystal clear stream. Nawakwa killed a young fawn and they roasted it to a golden brown and had a delicious feast. Afterwards, White Loon shredded a small piece of tobacco into the palm of his left hand and sprinkled a few grains on the embers. His lips moved and his eyes were closed as if in prayer. Then, mixing the rest of the tobacco with a few dried sumac leaves taken from his bullet pouch, he filled the bowl of his tomahawk, which also served as a pipe, and smoked several puffs before handing it over to Nawakwa.

"Hope it makes you sick, you old crow," said Jubal with a friendly smile. The good meal plus the knowledge they were not going to kill him made him bold and forgetful of last night's promise to his star.

"Onee," replied White Loon.

"You too, dirty face," he turned solemnly to the other. "Hope it kills you!" And he muffled a giggle. Inky would be awfully proud of him. The two had often talked about what they would do should either be captured by Injuns.

The two red men took turns smoking the pipe and watching the fire burn down. And Jubal was sound asleep long before they tied him up for the night.

He was awakened in the middle of the night by the thudding of his heart. A terrible roar filled his ears. He gasped for breath and dug his fingers into the earth, for some powerful force was trying to lift him bodily off the ground. Overhead, thunder crashed recklessly and the lightning was a steady, blinding glare of blue-white brilliance. It staggered earthward in vivid, crackling bolts from a mass of furiously twisting gray clouds. Jubal sprang up as far as his cord would permit, staring at the tempest in near panic. A wild wind screamed through the woods, filling the air with flying branches and even logs; in its whirlwind fury it picked up dead leaves and thorny twigs and hurled them into the boy's face. He looked for his captors and was shocked to see them standing close together, their faces raised to meet the wind, commenting in delighted wonder at the violence of the tornado. "Wawaugh! Waugh!" they exclaimed to each other as the lightning forked into a thousand dazzling branches and skipped from cloud to cloud in the churning skies. They shook their heads in admiration as each new peal of thunder roared across the heavens to shake the earth beneath them. Trembling, Jubal crouched down in a small hollow in the ground and pulled the blanket around his shoulders. He wondered what more could possibly happen to him. After what seemed an eternity the storm raged on toward the south. The wind died to a moan and the fierce lightning dwindled into pink flashes dancing in the distance.

Next morning the sun rose brilliantly above a cloudless horizon. The whole earth shone in scrubbed clarity. Had it not been for the bent tree tops and the fallen debris, Jubal would have thought the awesome night a bad dream. As they travelled north they had to climb over giant trees torn up by the roots, and where the full fury of the storm had struck, trees were twisted off above the root. Jubal was glad he had not been in the middle of such a storm.

With every passing day the boy thought of new plans for escape. But so closely did the two Indians watch him that he was seldom out of sight of one or the other. After six days of travel they reached a wide river Jubal later learned was the Auglaize, and it was here he saw the first of the Indian towns. They paused while White Loon cut a pole and tied the scalp to the end of it. Jubal shuddered at the sight of gray hair hanging from the long pole. It looked vaugely familiar but he didn't want to think about it. White Loon raised his prize over his head, waved it triumphantly in the air and gave a series of shrill whoops as they entered the town.

A large crowd of men, women and children gathered around the two braves and their white prisoner. After many welcoming speeches they all sat gravely down, some on logs, others on the ground, to listen to the Loon tell the story of Jubal's capture, and of how he had scalped a man earlier that same day. The Indian fondled his deerskin package, and by his gestures and sign language Jubal guessed it was a gift for someone very important — and had been taken from the scalped one.

White Loon had scarcely ended his tale when without warning a bent, gnome-like old Indian jumped up, gave a terrible scream and threw himself upon Jubal, knocking the boy to the ground. The red man's wrinkled, brown face was contorted in a fearsome grimace and his beady eyes glowed with hatred. Babbling in his native tongue, he raised a claw-like fist as if to beat the life out of his victim.

COOH-COO-CHEEH

"Oh, Pa, Ma, say goodbye to your only son!" thought Jubal, his heart thudding with fear.

Swiftly White Loon moved forward with one powerful blow struck the old man aside, shouting angrily in Shawanese. Then he picked Jubal up in his strong arms and the three left the village in silence, once again heading north. At nightfall they shot a large hawk, and after carefully plucking out its feathers they boiled the bird in a brass kettle with milk-weed. It was the most sickening soup Jubal had ever eaten, and the meat was so tough he could hardly swallow it. He spent the night tossing restlessly between his two captors; great spasms of grinding pain rose up from his stomach until he thought he would die.

About noon the next day they came to a village on the point of land where the Auglaize joined the Maumee River. In spite of the sharp pains in his stomach, Jubal thought it was the most beautiful place he had ever seen. A small village of a dozen or so log houses surrounded by thick oak woods hugged the shore of the river. The two Indians led him down a dusty street until they reached a long, low building of hewed logs that seemed to house three separate store rooms. A big, pleasant looking white man stood in the narrow doorway.

"Well, well," he boomed when he saw Jubal, "what have we here?"

A white man! A vague hope sprang up in the weary captive's breast. "I'm Jubal Hewitt — from Columbia," he blurted out. "These varmints captured me on the way home from Fort Washington — oh Sir, could you make them let me go home?"

The big man eyed him kindly. "I'm afraid not, son," he replied, "but I can give you a few pointers on how to behave."

Jubal sighed and wished his stomach would stop hurting. "My folks tried to do that," he said, "but I don't seem to learn very well."

The man laughed. "Sit down, lad. It'll take the better part of the afternoon to sort these fur pelts White Loon brought in. Tell me more about your family and how you happen to be here."

He listened sympathetically while Jubal poured out his tale. Then he said, "I'm afraid you'll have to get used to living with us for the time being. The Indians will want a ransom from your folks — or else you will have to work out the price of your own ransom if your people can't pay."

"I hope their old ransom isn't too high," said Jubal glumly, "cause my folks sure can't pay much."

"Well, Jubal Hewitt, I'm George Ironside, trader and British Indian agent." He stood up and motioned for the boy to follow him to the open door. "Come here, lad. Since you're going to live among us you might as well start getting acquainted with the town now. See that farthest house near the river? Belongs to Henry Ball, an American captured at St. Clair's defeat, and his wife Polly Meadows. They're allowed to live there and work out their ransom price; Henry by boating to the rapids of the Maumee and Polly by sewing." He paused to wave to a small, dark man with a pointed mustache.

"That's Perault, the baker. He's French — lives right next door. Over there is M'Kenzie, a silversmith and a rascal. And across from me," he nodded toward two cabins enclosed by a stockade, "those two places belong to the Girty brothers, Simon and James."

Jubal shivered. He had heard many tales of the bloody renegade Girty brothers. "Who lives in that house across the river?"

"That's where Cooh-coo-cheeh lives. She's the mother of White Loon. Sort of the High Priestess of the tribes. By the way, be careful of Nawakwa — he's a mean devil."

"And all those smaller cabins?"

"Oh, other French and English families."

Jubal shivered again. Here he was, miles from home, surrounded by the British enemy, prisoner of the Indian enemy. Whatever would become of him? George Ironside read his thoughts and laughed heartily. "It's not all that bad, Jubal Hewitt," he said. "You will receive fair treatment from the Indians. And we English do not eat white boys — at least not yet!"

Just then White Loon entered the warehouse, and the trader paid him a raft of silver trinkets for his skins. Nawakwa had gone. White Loon beckoned to Jubal. "Come," he said, "I take you to new home."

Jubal stood up — then gave a startled little jump. This Injun spoke English! His scalp prickled as he remembered some of his remarks on the trip north. He wondered why they had not killed him then. White Loon's eyes were bright with suppressed laughter.

"Big joke on small paleface — yes?" he said.

"Yes...no...er —" stammered Jubal, his face scarlet.

"Small brave talk big on trail. Good for you Nawakwa not understand. Him have hot temper — scalp quick!" he ran a forefinger around Jubal's hairline.

George Ironside chuckled. "White Loon likes his little joke," he told Jubal. "Most of these Indians do. Well, goodbye, Jubal Hewitt. We shall see more of each other."

After crossing the Maumee in a canoe, the stocky Indian and his white prisoner started up a grassy slope toward the bark cabin Jubal had seen from Ironside's warehouse. It was a neat appearing house, somewhat larger than those in the town. A big gray-brown dog snoozed in the open doorway. White Loon stooped to scratch his ears and the animal waved his shaggy tail lazily without opening his eyes. Then, grasping Jubal firmly by the wrist, the Loon led the boy into the dim house and presented him to an ancient squaw. Her stout shoulders were bent with age and her bronze face a mass of fine wrinkles, but her black eyes were bright and clear and snapping with hostility. She was dressed in a shirt of yellow calico that hung out over a blue stroud and was fastened at her throat with a massive silver brooch. Her legs were encased in a pair of blue leggings and her moccasins brightly trimmed with ribbons and porcupine quills. Heavy silver bracelets covered her arms. The White Loon gave Jubal a shove in the Ancient One's direction and spoke sharply to her in Shawanese.

The woman replied by baring her teeth in a snarl. "Me no want man child!" she snapped in broken English.

The White Loon ignored her and said to Jubal, "This Coohcoo-cheeh. You work for her — she take care of you." And with no further ado he stalked out of the house, leaving Jubal alone with the old squaw.

She looked him up and down slowly, noting the scratches on his dirty face, the torn clothes on his thin body and his swollen, bleeding feet. "You look like plucked turkey," she exclaimed, her nostrils quivering. "Smell like goat."

Weak from weariness, sick from the Indian food, Jubal felt a great surge of bitterness at being here at all. "That's from bein' with you Injuns so long," he flared.

The old woman frowned at him for a long minute. Then she broke out into sudden laughter. "You may be all-right at that," she said. "I keep! You work for Cooh-coo-cheeh! Come!" she offered him a hand. "We bathe."

Leading Jubal to the river, she scrubbed him clean, then made him lie down on a blanket while she washed his clothes. She "oohed" and "aahed" as she felt the soft silk of his vest and saw the plate buttons. "You wear fine clothes. Come from rich people — pay big ransom," she gloated. She filled a large copper kettle with water, threw in a handful of dewberry root, the bark of a wild cherry tree and of a red oak tree, and brewed a hot tea for Jubal to drink. "Make stomach stop hurting," she told him.

"How'd you know my stomach hurt?" queried Jubal.

"Cooh-coo-cheeh know much. Very wise."

She made him soak his feet in the tea he did not drink, and, to his surprise, both his stomach and his feet felt much better. She took him back to her house, where she cut green corn from the cob, pounding it until it resembled thick cream. Pouring the mixture into an oblong mold made of corn leaves, she baked it in hot ashes until it was a crusty brown on the outside and custardy inside. She slapped a great heaping spoonful of the pudding into a wooden bowl, handed it to Jubal along with a pewter spoon and ordered him to eat it all.

"Make little Sawendebans better," she said.

"My name's Jubal, ma'am. Jubal Hewitt," said Jubal politely.

"You Sawendebans!" she glared fiercely at him. "It mean Yellow Hair."

"Yes'm." Jubal agreed, wolfing down his corn dish. He would be as polite as he could, for surely a party from Fort Washington would soon come for him.

Cooh-coo-cheeh chatted as he ate and a shaggy dog nuzzled around his feet, its tail wagging slowly. "Him Blowing Snow," she nodded toward the pet. "Me Princess of Wolf

Tribe of mighty Iroquois Nation." She went on to tell Jubal of her husband, a powerful Mohawk chief who had been killed fighting against General Harmar three years past. "Him buried up there," she pointed to a red post standing at the top of the hill. "Up there, where me talk to him, where him watch warriors cross Maumee on warpath. Him buried sitting up, facing west. Come, you see." She left the house, gesturing for Jubal to come along.

Jubal followed the old Princess to the post on the crest of the hill. It was painted a bright red, and near its top was the carved image of a human face. Below the face was marked the number of scalps the chief had taken in battle, and below this were the scalps, streaming in the breeze. Jubal felt nauseated. He counted nineteen in all, and knew all nineteen had belonged to his people. He was reminded of White Loon brandishing a scalp upon entering the first Shawnee town. Again came the vague feeling of recognition.

"Now," Cooh-coo-cheeh started down the slope. "Little brave sleep."

The bark house of Cooh-coo-cheeh was larger than the Hewitt cabin on the banks of the Ohio. Its frame was made of small poles placed upright in the ground that served as eave-bearers, while others, firmly tied to the poles by thongs of hickory bark, formed girders and rafters. Large slabs of dried elm bark made the outside walls and roof of the cabin. Inside were two separate apartments divided by a bark partition, one apparently a pantry and the other a living room. Around three walls of the living room ran fur pelts and bright red blankets, providing seats by day and beds, if needed, by night. On the ground in the center of the room was a firepit and over it, suspended from a ridge pole, hung a wooden pot for cooking. A large brass kettle, a few knives, tin cups, pewter and horn spoons, sieves, wooden bowls and baskets of various sizes, a block for making hominy, four beds and a copper kettle made up the old Princess's household furnishings. The rooms were clean and tidy.

Cooh-coo-cheeh helped Jubal climb up on the platform and with surprising tenderness laid one of the red blankets over him, muttering all the while that she did not want another man child.

The first few weeks of his new life Jubal was too busy working for the old squaw to be lonely. He carried water from the river up the steep hill to the cabin. He gathered corn from the fields, ground it with a mortar, and washed the hominy after she had boiled it over hot ashes. He cleaned the fish her many friends from the village brought. And by the time the sun dropped behind the river, he was happy to stretch out on one of her beds and fall into a dreamless slumber.

However, many times during the long summer days he had time to explore on his own. From the top of their hill he could see more than a mile up the Auglaize River. The river banks appeared to be one continuous village as far as his eye could see. At the point where the Auglaize mingled its current with the Maumee the water whirled and eddied in powerful pools. On the high ground stood beautiful open woods of oak and hickory, while a tangled mass of berry bushes, saplings, blue and white ash trees and elms covered the bottomlands below. On the south side of the Maumee, extending so far that it disappeared in shimmering waves of heat, stretched a vast corn field, now in tassle. Apple and peach orchards covered the hills beyond the river. Every day Jubal saw Indian boys about his own age shooting fish in the river with bow and arrows. He wondered whether he would ever get to know them.

Several times a week, warriors from the village crossed the river to visit Cooh-coo-cheeh. They always brought her gifts; a side of venison or a haunch of bear meat, soft otter or beaver pelts, or the small silver brooches she loved so well. Jubal was a little frightened by the appearance of the braves. They wore silver gorgets and medallions around their necks, silver rings in their noses and heavy pieces of silver in their pierced ears. Sometimes they were vividly painted, sometimes not.

"What are those big silver medals they wear, Cooh-coo-cheeh? And who is the man on them?" asked Jubal one day after a richly dressed group had left.

"Those medallions of King George Third, British father across big water," replied Cooh-coo-cheeh. "That picture of British father; him send many presents to his red children."

Jubal snorted. No wonder the Injuns were loyal to the Crown. Always getting gifts from the British!

And while never a day passed that he didn't think of his family, still he was not unhappy. The old Princess was more kindhearted than she meant to be. She nursed him back to health until he grew plump and red-cheeked. Sometimes she asked about his mother and tried to comfort him with clucking sounds and a huge bowl of pumpkin stewed with maple sugar. He learned to obey her and to watch for signs of her quick, fierce temper, which flared briefly but dangerously. Blowing Snow was forever at his heels. At night the big old animal crept in bed beside Jubal and was a great comfort to the boy.

One morning Cooh-coo-cheeh wakened Jubal before sunrise. "Come, Sawendebans," she said, shaking him violently. "You get dressed! Today very busy — we pick up Quasay, then visit Blue Jacket!"

BLUE JACKET'S TOWN

Blue Jacket, second in power only to the celebrated Little Turtle, dressed with care. He must look his best this morning, for he was to have his portrait painted by the young painter-man who lived among them now for nearly four months. And was it not to be sent to hang in the lodge of the British father in London? And this afternoon he was to receive Black Snake, a chief from a neighboring village. Blue Jacket stooped to look at himself in an oblong mirror hanging on the wall. The image he saw pleased him, large piercing gray eyes set wide apart under a high, broad forehead, straight, aquiline nose, and wide mouth. His intelligent face was deeply tanned yet much lighter than his Indian brothers — but that was Blue Jacket's secret and he hardly ever thought of it anymore. Most of those who shared the secret with him were now in the Happy Hunting, and the few who remained had forgotten. "Yes," he told the image in the mirror, "it is a better life than you could have had farming the stony fields of Pennsylvania!"

"What are you saying, Blue Jacket?" his French Canadian wife entered the room. "Eh bien! You are splendide! Tres elegante!"

He smiled at her. "Place the King's Medallion over my head," he said.

The woman obeyed, then stood back to admire her husband. Blue Jacket was magnificent in a scarlet frock coat richly laced with gold and tied around the waist with a bright sash. He wore red leggings and his moccasins were ornamented with glittering designs. Gold epaulets covered each shoulder, and around his neck hung the George Medallion along with another larger silver gorget.

The woman peeked out of the lodge. "The painterman is here," she said.

The chief took one more look at himself, straightened to his full six feet and swung out of the lodge. The artist was waiting with a large piece of tent canvas stretched over a smooth board, his oil paints in a circle around him.

"Mr. Alexander Keene," Blue Jacket greeted him in perfect English. "I have heard much of your great talent."

Alex blinked, his heart beating a little faster. What a splendid painting this handsome, colorful Indian would make! His fingers itched to get to work.

"Blue Jacket is kind," he replied, mentally placing the chief against a background of dark green hemlocks, touched here and there with golden sunlight. He must have a fine weapon in one hand. Alex's eyes searched the front of the lodge, where many firearms were displayed.

"You have painted many landscapes," Blue Jacket persisted, his gray eyes shrewd. "Many from the tops of hills. Why is this?"

Alex levelled his gaze at the Indian. Here was no ordinary savage. "Every artist has his own way of painting," he replied evenly. "I like to paint the land as it must appear to the Great Manitou. It fills me with wonder to paint billowing oceans of green trees cut here and there by silver streams. Do you understand, Blue Jacket?"

Blue Jacket ignored his question. "How shall I pose?" he asked.

Once again Alex let his gaze travel over the front of the lodge. Many rifles, war clubs, bows and arrows and other implements of war adorned the elm-bark lodge. The skins of deer and bear, otter and panther were stretched as a record of the chief's hunting prowess. "There is not a weapon there rich enough to be in the same painting with you, Blue Jacket," he declared. "I see you resting after the hunt, the forest dark and brooding behind you, forced to reveal its secrets to so great a hunter." Alex was being over eloquent and he knew it, but the Indian seemed to like it and it kept him from asking too many questions. "Never mind, I'll paint in a fancy rifle later. Would you go over and sit down on that log?"

Blue Jacket obeyed. "White Loon is bringing me a scalp and some gifts this afternoon from his latest raid south. Maybe he will bring a gun."

"I'm glad I'm a simple painter and not mixed up in your wars," remarked Alex, thinning a daub of sienna paint with linseed oil. With a large, white-tipped goose quill brush he began to sketch rapidly.

The Indian frowned. "It was decided at Council last week. If the Americans want a firm and lasting peace, they must immediately remove all their people from this side of the Ohio River. All lands north of the river belong to the Indian!"

"And to the British father," agreed Alex. "He will help if it comes to war."

"He is helping us now," asserted Blue Jacket. "Our great father will unite with us in war and drive the pale faces from the land they have unjustly stolen from the red man."

"You speak English well," Alex changed the subject. He could not afford to give way to his anger now. He had many maps rolled up in his pack. He wondered what had happened to his amazing contact. He had not seen him for over two weeks. Had he been discovered? Was that why this gray-eyed

Indian chief asked so many questions about his paintings? Alex knew that Wayne would soon be ready to start north from Hobson's Choice and would need the maps to lay out his wide roads.

The morning wore on, growing hotter as the sun rose higher in the sky. Curious Indians from the town sauntered by and lingered to watch the artist work. Alex painted with swift, sure strokes, blocking in the deep green of the forest, then the bronze face with dark umber shadows and finally the joyous red of the gaudy costume. A thin wash of cobalt would be enough sky for the time being. It was turning into the best portrait Alex had ever painted, and his excitement ran high as he worked. If this business in the Northwest would ever come to a head, he would return to fetch Polly from Columbia, then head east and set up a studio of his own. He glanced up in annoyance as an Indian strolled too near and jostled his arm.

"Watch it!" he snapped.

The Indian's black eyes flicked over the painter vacantly and he strolled on toward the woods. Alex gave an inward sigh of relief.

"Would you like to rest?" he asked at length.

"Blue Jacket has no need to rest," retorted the chief.

And they both fell silent.

"Who is Quasay?" queried Jubal as he trotted alongside the old princess through the cool green forest. Blowing Snow pranced ahead, sniffing the wonderful scents of chipmunks and raccoons on the mossy path.

"Quasay grandchild of Cooh-coo-cheeh," replied the woman. "She always spend winter with Cooh-coo-cheeh. Playmate for Sawendebans."

Jubal sniffed, remembering the Foster girls. "Blowing Snow's enough playmate for me," he said.

"Him old. No playmate," she scoffed, gently nudging the dog with her toe.

"He's better'n any old girl," muttered Jubal.

"Not better than Quasay!" Cooh-coo-cheeh's quick temper flared and she swung a blow at Jubal, which he saw coming and ducked. But she became cheerful again immediately. "Here is house of White Loon." She took him to a roomy bark house built at the very edge of the river.

White Loon had already left for Blue Jacket's Town with his presents for the chief, but his pretty young wife greeted them pleasantly. Quasay proved to be a small Indian girl about Jubal's own age. She had a slim wiry body and a heart-shaped face with large black eyes that slanted up at the corners, giving her an odd elfin look. She was dressed in a bright blue stroud trimmed with red ribbons and edged around the hem with multi-colored beads. Her brown legs were bare. Fastened to her moccasins were small tufts of deer hair, dyed red and confined in tiny cones of tin that rattled as she walked. Wide silver bracelets clanked on her arms and gleaming silver brooches decorated her waist. She danced gaily out of the cabin at Cooh-coo-cheeh's call, but stopped short at the sight of the strange white boy.

"Who is that?" she asked, staring coldly at Jubal.

"This is Sawendebans, new brother for Quasay," answered Cooh-coo-cheeh.

"I no want new brother!" snapped Quasay.

"Well, you got one!" Cooh-coo-cheeh glared at her granddaughter.

Quasay glared back, a younger version of the old Princess, but kept quiet.

Quasay's mother served them a meal of green corn boiled with beans and dried pumpkin. Then, after a brief rest, they started up the path to Blue Jacket's Town.

A large, brightly garbed crowd of Indians milled in front of Blue Jacket's lodge that hot smoky day in early August. As Cooh-coo-cheeh and the two children approached, the people clustered around them to admire Jubal's golden hair. To his embarrassment the women patted his head and rubbed strands of his hair through their fingers, chattering excitedly.

"Blue Jacket very busy today," said one young squaw. "Him being painted!"

"And Black Snake soon come to visit," chimed in another.

Cooh-coo-cheeh grabbed the boy and girl each by a hand and pulled them through the crowd. "We get closer," she grumbled. "Cannot see over heads of many people!"

Alex had finished for the day. He could do no more until parts of his painting dried. At Blue Jacket's command he was seated on an otter skin smoking a pipe, his keen eyes observing everything. Suddenly, in the center of the curious crowd of people, he spotted a head of yellow hair. They had captured a white child, he thought, a great wave of anger rising in him. He rose to a half crouch — then saw the child's face. He blinked, unable to believe what he saw. It could not be — and yet it was! Jubal! Jubal Hewitt, Polly's brother!

At that same moment Jubal's eager gaze, sweeping the half-circle of men seated before Blue Jacket's lodge, focussed on Alex. He froze on the spot. Then with a glad cry, he broke away from Cooh-coo-cheeh and made a blind dive toward the painterman. "Alex! Alex! Alex!" he cried, tears of joy running down his cheeks. "I *knew* you were alive!"

"Jube!" The two embraced each other while the Indians watched in grave silence.

"How do you know this boy?" asked Blue Jacket.

"Came downriver together," answered Alex.

"We sure did!" cried Jubal, all smiles. " 'Till the Injuns — er, you Injuns got him right off the boat! I'm sure glad to see you, Alex."

Alexander Keene smiled, but he was sick at heart. The appearance of Polly's little brother was something for which he had not bargained.

They were interrupted by sharp scalp yells. It was White Loon, plumed and painted in his best war dress. Blue Jacket held up a hand for silence and began to speak in Shawanese.

"What's he saying, Alex?" asked Jubal.

"White Loon is going to present his great chief — ah — with gifts from his trip to the beautiful river," Alex translated. "That must've been when they picked you up, Jube."

White Loon was very dramatic, acting out how he and Naw-akwa had made their way to a new settlement to steal horses. There, in the dusk, they had come upon a lone man working late in the cornfields. With his hunting knife the Loon gave a convincing charade of the scalping. Then he presented the gray scalp to Blue Jacket, along with an object wrapped in deerskin. Blue Jacket graciously accepted the gift and proceeded to open it in front of the waiting crowd. As he threw back the wrapping, the sun caught and shone brightly on the polished brass mounts of a snub-nose pistol. Blue Jacket's eyes glittered. Turning to Alex, he said, "You see. It came. Is it right for the portrait?"

"Perfect, just perfect, Blue Jacket." Alex was sickened by the whole performance.

Jubal, at Alex's side, stood on tiptoe to better see the gun. Then he gave a terrible cry as he caught sight of the maple stock and the scroll-work monogram — I.A.F.!

Now he knew to whom the bushy gray scalp had belonged!

THE FEAST
OF THE
GREEN CORN

"Alex!" cried Jubal, "that pistol belonged to Increase Foster! The varmits killed him! He never hurt anybody in his life!" Jubal could recall many times when Increase Foster had been the only human being with a kind word for the harumscarum Hewitt boy. "The varmits!"

"Jubal!" There was a harsh note in Alex's voice. "Stop carryin' on. You're almost a man now — so start acting like one! You're a white prisoner in the heart of Indian Country and you're likely to see worse'n this before you ever lay eyes on your Ma and Pa again!"

"But — you liked him too, Alex."

"I liked him, sure. But things you can't change you have to face up to!"

Jubal gave his old friend a long, searching look. Alex had changed, he decided. Some of the gaiety had gone from his blue eyes and new worry lines had formed around his firm mouth. "Alex, why can't you and I escape? The two of us could figure out a way!"

The renegade, Simon Girty, who had been shamelessly eavesdropping, broke into an ugly laugh. "He's no prisoner, boy!"

Alex ignored him. "Go home with Cooh-coo-cheeh, Jubal. She's a friend of mine, so I'll be around to see you. Uh, Jube — how's Polly?"

"Fine, last time I saw her," Jubal replied vaguely. He was confused. He wanted to go to the lodge of Cooh-coo-cheeh and think about the day's events, and about what Simon Girty had said. Jubal had seen the painterman captured by the Indians. Yet this shaggy-haired, shifty-eyed renegade said Alex was not a prisoner! If — if he was not a prisoner, why then, did he not go back to get Polly? A sickening thought came to Jubal. What if Em Foster had been right and Alex was a spy for the British? "I won't think about it," he said to himself. "Everyone knows that Girty person is a turncoat and a liar!"

And Jubal could not brood long in the presence of the cheerful Quasay. Small-boned and agile, with a quick wit and a high tinkling laugh, Quasay brought gaiety to the lodge of her grandmother. Even white-jowled old Blowing Snow returned to his puppyhood at her being there. Every morning the dog wakened her by taking her slender wrists between his great jaws and gently pulling until she arose and romped with him. Her brief jealousy of Jubal was overcome by a greater love of teasing him.

"Come," she grabbed Jubal's hand one evening after supper. "I teach you to dance, Sawendebans."

"Not me," Jubal was busy stringing a bow.

"You must be ready for the Feast of the Green Corn," she insisted, pulling him up with all her strength.

"Quasay, go 'way!" croaked Jubal, "I ain't gonna dance!"

"Oogh!" Cooh-coo-cheeh swung a poker at him. "You dance, Yellow Hair!"

After a month of life with the old Princess, Jubal had discovered that while she was kind most of the time, her primitive temper was always close to the surface and when roused was like a fury. Nor was she particular in selecting an instrument of punishment. When her poker was not at hand she seized a knife, piece of wood, or anything within her reach and hurled it at the object of her wrath. Jubal glared at her and allowed Quasay to begin his dancing lessons. First with one foot then the other, he had to step forward lightly, then gracefully sink with a rocking motion, spring up briskly and lope into a galloping trot. The last step Jubal excuted so awkwardly that Quasay rolled on the ground with laughter as Cooh-coo-cheeh muttered something about clumsy pale-faces.

One hot evening when the smoke from the campfires across the river blurred the horizon with shades of blue, Jubal showed Quasay and her grandmother a dance he had watched Polly learn in the east. "This, mesdames, is the Double Chasse'," he mimicked the dancing master. They laughed so hard that he went from the Chasse' into a vigorous hornpipe, singing at the top of his lungs.

"Very good, lad!" cried a fimiliar voice when he finally threw himself onto to the ground, panting for breath.

"Alex!" gasped Jubal, jumping up to greet his friend.

"You come to paint Cooh-coo-cheeh and Quasay for British Father?" asked Quasay, dancing around the painterman.

"He come to build shed for Cooh-coo-cheeh," the princess corrected her. "Need room to sit guests for Green Corn Dance."

If Jubal had hoped to talk alone with the painterman, he was disappointed. Alex worked swiftly putting up the three-sided bark shed that would house the more aged of Cooh-coo-cheeh's visitors. Every day some one from the village came over to give advice, and Jubal noticed how friendly Alex was with these Englishmen. George Ironside seemed to be one of his best friends — but then, George Ironside was everybody's friend. On his first visit he greeted Jubal with a loud cry. "Well, well lad, I see the Ancient One has cast one of her magic spells over you and put some fat on your bones!" he boomed.

"No magic spells, Mr. Ironside," grinned Jubal. "Just plenty of venison stew and maple sugared pumpkin." Much later Jubal learned that the trader was a graduate of King's College in Aberdeen, and had served for many years in the British Indian Department.

Often John M'Kenzie, the silversmith who exchanged silver ornaments at an enormous profit for skins and furs, would spend the morning regaling them with his hilarious tales of his life on the frontier. Alex seemed his former merry self, laughing and joking with his British friends. But he was careful never to be alone with Jubal.

One pleasant morning in the middle of August, when the ears of corn were full grown yet in the soft, milky state best for roasting, Quasay and Blowing Snow were up earlier than usual.

"Sawendebans," crooned the girl in her musical voice, "you lazy raccoon, get up! Today is the Feast of the Green Corn!"

"Go 'way," mumbled Jubal.

"Here, Blowing Snow — here is new wrist for you to eat!" Quasay placed Jubal's arm in the dog's mouth and pressed his great jaws together until Jubal yiped in pain.

"Ouch! Quasay, you're not like any girl I ever knew before! You're too rough!" He leapt from his bed.

The smile faded from Quasay's pixie face and she threw him an an odd look as she ran from the cabin to fetch water. The house of Cooh-coo-cheeh was spotless and her kettles shining by mid-morning, when her guests began to arrive. Two of her three sons and their wives, George Ironside with his Indian wife, Bad Bird, Nawakwa, Alex, several Shawnee warriors and a few old squaws were Cooh-coo-cheeh's guests for the day.

The Indians greeted each other politely, then seated themselves on the grass and passed a pipe three or four times. At length a fat Indian stood up and began to speak.

"What's he sayin', Quasay?" asked Jubal. He had learned a little of the Shawanese language, but not enough to understand a speech. "And who is he? I saw him in Grand Glaize that day."

"Him Round-as-a-Pumpkin," explained the girl. "Him Delaware Indian who escaped from the Gnadenhutten massacre. Him say, 'Thank you, Great spirit, for giving Indian such wonderful country that give such wonderful harvest. Indian thank you by feasting on Your bounty and by sporting.' " She paused to listen, then continued. "Him say, 'Paleface are murderers. Indian defeat of St. Clair show returning favor of Great Spirit — Manitou now smiles on his red children. Palefaces shall never plant corn north of Ohio River!' " She looked impishly at Jubal. "You Paleface murderer. You plant corn north of Ohio River!" She gave him a playful slap on the back that sent him tumbling down the hill and almost into the river.

"Quasay — " he clambered back up, ready to return the blow, when one of the warriors gave a prolonged whoop. This signalled the beginning of the sports. First was a footrace, won by one of Cooh-coo-cheeh's sons, Black Loon. The race was followed by wrestling matches, with ugly-faced Nawakwa the undisputed champion. After downing three muscular braves, he turned unexpectedly to Alex.

"You next," he shouted in Shawanese.

"Not me," Alex shook his head.

"You paleface coward!" sneered Nawakwa.

The crowd sucked in its breath and waited in silence. Alex's tanned face turned pale under the taunt, and he jumped to his feet. Unstrapping his pack, he handed it to Jubal for safekeeping, then crouched to meet his tormentor.

There was hardly a sound from the circle of Indians. All eyes were fixed on the two powerful figures moving catlike around each other in the center of the circle. A light breeze whispered through the leafy branches of the hickory trees and danced across the glistening faces of the contestants. For a few minutes the Indian and the white man cagily tested each other's strength and skill. Neither uttered a word as they grappled, carefully at first, then more violently, until they were locked in a muscular embrace. Breaking loose, Alex lifted the Indian from his feet and tried to throw him, but the red man was too skillful. With a swift writhing movement of his supple body he bent Alex painfully backward toward the ground.

"He'll kill Alex," whispered Jubal to Quasay.

Quasay's black eyes were wide, "Nawakwa like to kill," she murmured.

Alex wriggled out of Nawakwa's iron grip and shook his head as a dog might, to clear his mind. Nawakwa took advantage of the painterman's unguarded movement and, with a trip of his foot and a swift twist of his body, threw the white man furiously to the earth. Alex, his eyes narrowed, his breath coming in painful gasps, sprang back to his feet. Like a panther he slithered across the dust and seized the Indian around his middle. Nawakwa glowered, twisting his moist body in a vain effort to free himself. Alex, his face scarlet from exertion and anger, slowly raised the brave on his hip and held him there for a breathless moment. Then, with one last mighty burst of strength, he pitched the snarling Indian head over heels through the air. Nawakwa landed with an explosive thud on his back. For several minutes he lay there, rolling from side to side dazedly and sobbing for air.

The crowd murmured, "Waugh!" and Alex headed for the river to splash his burning face. Nawakwa slunk off into the hickory woods to lick his wounds in private. "Quasay glad the paleface won," confided the girl to Jubal as they prepared to eat the feast Cooh-coo-cheeh had prepared.

There was boiled jerky and fish, stewed squirrel and venison — and plenty of green corn, some boiled on the ear and some cut from the cob and mixed with beans to make succotash. There was corn bread baked crisp and golden, squash and roasted pumpkin; juicy wild grapes, sweet tasting peaches and tart plums. When they had eaten all they could, the men passed the pipe again and Cooh-coo-cheeh brought out a small keg of rum.

"You, Sawendebans and Quasay, you gather up all weapons before Black Loon open firewater," ordered the princess. "Then warriors no kill each other and dirty up land of Cooh-coo-cheeh!" She chuckled to one of her old squaw friends.

The afternoon passed pleasantly. Some of the guests engaged in a tug-of-war with a long piece of rawhide. Others sat sipping the warm rum and chatting. And when the dipping sun sent long blue shadows over the hillside, the dancing began. The men moved with their rocking motion in a circle, and the women danced in a smaller circle inside. A wizened old man beat out a primitive rhythm with a stick on a small drum and sang. Quasay joined the women, and Jubal danced one full circle to please Cooh-coo-cheeh, then dropped out.

He wondered where Alex was. The painterman would have to return for his pack. Jubal lifted it off the ground three or four times. It seemed awfully heavy — there must be many paintings inside. He carried it to the edge of the woods and placed it beside a dead oak for safekeeping, then sat down to rest. He could see that the dance was going well. No one was drinking too much rum. He looked again at Alex's pack. Finally, his curiosity getting the best of him, Jubal opened the flap and peeked inside. There were several canvases rolled up, a great many oil colors, some dried madder root and three brushes — one tipped with Thankful's tail. Jubal grinned to himself, remembering that windy day on the banks of the Youghiogheny. He unrolled the first canvas. It was a striking portrait of the Indian chief, Blue Jacket, with the words "To the British Father" lettered neatly underneath. The next was of another Indian chief whom Jubal had never seen, titled

"Buckhongelas." The rest were landscapes. Jubal studied them in the waning light. They looked like landscapes — yet different. They were more like maps! That was it, maps! Slowly Jubal rolled the canvases back up and replaced them in the pack. He felt ill. If the portraits were meant for the British father, why the maps must be too!

A shrill scream from the group around the campfire caused him to drop the pack and head for the dancers.

"Painterman! Painterman! Look out!" It was Quasay's frantic warning.

A GREAT HUNTER

Jubal shouldered through the crowd in time to see Alex bent over the fire roasting a piece of venison, Nawakwa behind him with a raised tomahawk. At Quasay's frightened shriek, the painterman leapt to one side and rolled out of the Indian's reach. The enraged Nawakwa, his teeth bared in an ugly snarl, started after his prey. With agility surprising in one so heavy, Round-as-a-Pumpkin threw out a foot and tripped the angry warrior.

"There has been enough killing," he exclaimed, wrestling the axe from Nawakwa's hand. "Cooh-coo-cheeh, send them home, The Feast is over!"

Cooh-coo-cheeh bade her guests goodbye. The fat Indian was the last to leave. Before he did, he placed a hand on Jubal's yellow head. "I had a friend once," he said, "a little white boy like you. Only he had black hair —" he stopped, seemingly overcome by the turn of events, and hurried away into the night.

"Where'd you put my pack, Jube?" asked Alex.

"Over there," Jubal gave him an unfriendly stare and pointed to the dead oak.

Alex hesitated. "You looked inside," he said accusingly.

"Yup."

"That was wrong of you."

"Yup. What you're doin' is wrong too."

Alex gave Jubal a hard look. "That depends on how you look at it — which side you're standin' on," he said at length.

"Well, now I know which side *you're* standin' on," flared Jubal. "I hope the British father will like your paintin's, Mr. Alexander Keene, 'cause none of us Americans will!" He stomped off to look for Quasay and Blowing Snow, leaving the painterman with a heavy sadness in his heart.

As late summer waned into autumn, the countryside took on a tawny glow. The sharp blue of the sky was reflected in the two rivers, turning them into ribbons of sapphire flowing between woods of brilliant yellow, crimson and copper. Many a bright day Jubal and Quasay took bows and arrows into the deep forest to hunt. Jubal became an expert at shooting birds. One day he shot a fat rabbit, which he proudly carried home to Cooh-coo-cheeh.

"You are a great hunter," she declared in delight.

Since the Feast of the Green Corn he had seen nothing of Alex, and he was glad. He felt Alex had betrayed them all — Pa, Ma and especially Polly, to say nothing of himself. They had given the limner their unquestioning friendship and here he was, aiding the Crown to carry out their destruction. First thing he must do when he returned to Columbia was to apologize to Em Foster.

With the approach of winter Cooh-coo-cheeh gave Jubal a new white shirt, a blanket coat, blue leggings and a bright waist-cloth. He looked like a bronze-skinned, yellow-haired Injun. In December, bone-chilling winds blew flurries of snow through the chinks of the house on the hill, and they kept a fire blazing night and day.

"You go get more wood, Sawendebans," the old squaw ordered one blustery afternoon.

"Shucks!" complained Jubal, who was stuffing his moccasins with tufts of deer hair for warmth.

"Yellow Hair want to freeze to death?" Cooh-coo-cheeh's black eyes flashed dangerously.

"No, ma'am," Jubal scrambled to his feet before she could reach her poker. "Come on, Quasay, let's go!"

"Quasay stay here," announced the girl. "If Quasay go, then Quasay chop wood while Paleface sit on log and give orders." She made a face at him. "Blowing Snow go."

"Shucks! Come on, old dog!" Blowing Snow was flat on his broad back so near the fire that the flames almost licked his leathery old nose.

Gathering an axe and a long strap for tying the logs together, Jubal shrugged into his heavy blanket and set out. The bitter cold almost took his breath away. A dry snow whirled in fitful gusts around the boy and the dog, and they braced themselves against the icy wind that screamed across the frozen river. Blowing Snow waddled along beside Jubal, sneezing and sending baleful looks up at him. Not another soul was abroad this gray winter day. Jubal muttered to himself as he slid down the hill and plodded on toward the frozen bottom. Once there, it did not take him long to find a likely-looking saplin, and he began to chop with such angry strokes that chips flew every which way. When he had cut as many logs as he could carry on his back, he tied them in a bundle and heaved it on his back.

"This'll hold 'em for a while," he growled. "C'mon, old doggie, let's go home."

But Blowing Snow was nowhere to be seen. Jubal wandered around the slushy bottom calling for the dog. Of all times for the dog to vanish, he thought, this bitterly raw day was the worst. Suddenly he heard a low, throaty snarl from far ahead. Letting the bundle of logs slide off his back he ran quickly across a frozen brook and up over a slight rise in the land.

There sat Blowing Snow near a small tree, his tail beating the ground with rapid, jerky thumps. The thick hair on his back was ruffled and stiff. Growling fiercely, he looked up toward the top of the tree, then back to Jubal. "What are you tryin' to tell me?" whispered the boy, kneeling down alongside his pet. He followed the dog's gaze up and saw crouched on the limb of the tree a large catlike animal with a dark reddish-grey coat, a snow-white underbelly and an oddly round head.

"That's just a cat," he laughed, stroking Blowing Snow's rigid back. "You look like Thankful," he remarked to the animal, "only you've grown some!"

He threw several small sticks at the big cat, which brought forth a threatening hiss. Searching the ground, he found a large rock. "This'll take card of Mr. Cat," he said to the excited dog. Taking careful aim, he heaved the rock with all his might. It struck the cat on its head with a loud "thwack!" The beast whined with pain and sprang to the earth a few scant feet from where Jubal was standing. Instantly Blowing Snow bared his fangs and lunged forward to seize the animal by its throat. But so fierce and powerful was the cat that brave old Blowing Snow was several times forced to let go his hold. Again and again he darted back after his prey, sometimes crouching to dodge the brute's swiftly thrusting claws, other times confusing it by racing around in mad circles. Snarling hatefully, the creature slapped at the dog's flanks until they were bleeding and raw.

"Blowing Snow — stop! You'll be killed!" Jubal was frightened for the first time.

But the old dog had no intention of quiting. He fought with greater caution. Backing away he waited for another chance to attack, then swift as an arrow, he sprang for the cat's throat. The beast paused, confused, and Jubal began to swing his axe. With one of his blind swings, he cracked the axe into the skull of the cat. It collapsed at once. Blowing Snow, panting and covered with blood, stood in triumph over his vanquished enemy. Suddenly realizing what he had done, he began to wag his tail and jump excitedly up on Jubal, his jaws open wide as if he were laughing.

"Good dog! Good doggie!" cried Jubal, patting the dog's head tenderly. "Let's take this — this whatever it is home and get you fixed up too!"

Before shouldering the beast he turned its limp form over several times. He judged it to be about four feet from nose to end of its tail. "I wonder if this critter might be a young panther," he said to the dog. Blowing Snow licked Jubal's hand and kept right on prancing. It was his finest hour. Proudly the boy and the dog marched home, scarcely feeling the cold at all.

Jubal gave a shrill yell as he entered the lodge of Cooh-coo-cheeh. "You should have come, Quasay!" he shouted, throwing the cat down near the fire. "You missed all the excitement! Poor little Quasay-stay-at-home!" He teased, knowing full well how the girl loved excitement.

The old Princess raised her hands in surprise and cried, "Waugh! Haugh-h! Pooshun!"

Quasay danced around the cat, her eyes shining. "It's a wildcat! Very fierce — Sawendebans very strong! Very brave!" she sang.

They made Jubal tell and retell the story of how he had killed the cat. Then Cooh-coo-cheeh spoke. "You grow to be great hunter, Sawendebans," she placed her forefingers together, the Shawnee symbol of marriage, and pointed to Quasay. "You shall have my granddaughter for wife when you are man!"

Jubal grinned at Quasay and waited for her answering "ugh!" But to his surprise, she blushed and turned her head away.

After that, winter set in hard. Daylight came late and left early. The sun, if it shone at all, was pale and watery. Snow covered the ground for days on end and the Maumee stayed frozen solid. They cut a hole in the ice for their drinking water. When they were not working for Cooh-coo-cheeh, Quasay and Jubal coasted down the hill and far out across the Maumee on a sled made of buffalo ribs. Blowing Snow, resting on his laurels, was content to snooze near the warmth of the fire with his ancient mistress. Through the long winter afternoons and evenings Cooh-coo-cheeh amused them with tales of bloody battles fought by her nation, the Iroquois, in a pine-scented land far to the north and east, of the strength and bravery of her departed husband, the Mohawk chieftain. She told of conversations with the animals and spirits, and of how she was able to foretell the future.

"What's gonna happen to me, Cooh-coo-cheeh?" asked Jubal "Will I ever see my Ma and Pa again?"

Cooh-coo-cheeh looked very wise. She rolled her eyes heavenward and called upon the spirits to give an answer. She chanted. Then she spoke. "Spirits say...Sawendebans..." she paused to leer at the wide-eyed children. "Sawendebans go to bed!" And she broke out into a merry laugh.

One bitterly cold morning Cooh-coo-cheeh rose long before daybreak. She planned to make hominy today, and must boil the corn with ashes to remove the hulls. She crooned a little tune as she worked, stirring the mixture often. At last the corn was ready to be cleansed from the ashes. "Oogh!" she grunted. "Two lazy raccoons get up! Much work to be done."

Quasay jumped up at once, but Jubal was too warm and cozy. He opened one eye and rolled over.

"Oogh!" Cooh-coo-cheeh's quick temper flared and she rapped his rear smartly with her poker.

"Ouch!" yiped Jubal, leaping up.

"You clean corn now! she shouted, swinging her weapon with deadly accuracy. "Hurry! Hurry!" she hustled the protesting boy off to the river with the kettle of corn and sieve before he could put on his moccasins.

Grumbling, Jubal scrambled down the hill and out onto the frozen river. He placed the sieve beside the waterhole and emptied the corn into it. Dipping up water in a small gourd, he poured it over the hominy and rubbed it well to remove the hulls. After working a short while, he became aware of sharp pains stabbing up from his poor, half-frozen bare feet. He felt ill and thought he might faint. He could endure it no longer! Then a happy idea flashed into his head. Gingerly he placed first one numbed foot then the other into the sieve of warm hominy. Oh! What sheer delight! He wriggled his toes joyously in the mushy warmth of the hominy.

"Sawendebans!" A furious scream come from Cooh-coo-cheeh as she dashed toward the river, pale with rage and brandishing her poker.

"Uh-oh!" Jubal saw this time she was in a blind frenzy. He yanked both feet out of the warmth and half slid, half stumbled across the ice until he reached the bank far from the angry squaw. Then he broke into a trot and headed for the safety of the dense woods. Better by far to risk meeting a pack of hungry wolves than to face Cooh-coo-cheeh in a rage. He knew of an old cave high on a steep hill overlooking Black Snake's Town. There he would remain until his misdeed was forgiven.

Before long he reached the massive outcropping of rock boulders that sheltered a roomy cave. He wrapped part of his blanket around his sore feet and settled back to wait. Usually an hour was enough for Cooh-coo-cheeh to forget what had made her angry. The wind had died down and the sun filtered through the fleecy clouds to warm the frozen earth. Trickles of water slithered down the long, pointed icicles that hung from the rough sides of the cave. From where Jubal sat he could see far out over the countryside. Tiny figures from Black Snake's Town were playing ice hockey on the river.

Farther along the shore were the snow-covered houses of Blue Jacket's Town. About two hundred feet below him, at the foot of the hill, stood a thick oak woods. Winter-brown leaves still clung to the gnarled, wide-spreading branches of the ancient trees.

The sudden glint of sunlight on metal from the shadows of the oak grove caught Jubal's eye, and he pulled himself closer to the edge of the cliff. At first he saw nothing, and decided it was his imagination. Then it flashed again, and all at once he saw two men walking out of the grove. They paused at the edge for a long time, talking earnestly. Both were dressed in the deerskin suit of the frontiersman. The stockier of the two limped a little as he walked and held one foot off the ground when he stood. A fur hat covered his hair, and a medallion shone on his breast. The silver medallion of the king, thought Jubal. Then the slender younger man handed over a large package from the pack on his back and the two nodded and left, going in opposite directions.

"I wonder who the man wearing the medallion was," thought Jubal bitterly. The other he knew well. It was Alexander Keene.

RUMORS

The two men in the oak woods spoke in hushed tones as they pored over Alex's paintings.

"Your first maps were wonderous good, Alex," said Anthony Wayne, his hazel eyes alight in his drawn face. "The Legion cut roads sixty feet wide beyond Fort Jefferson, thanks to you. We built Greenville where you suggested — gad, man! What is this gruesome masterpiece? he asked, staring at one of the paintings.

Alex looked grim. "Sir, this is the land of the dead! The bones of St. Clair's men are still unburied — I thought on your way north it might be Christian to stop and bury them. Now this —" he ruffled through the canvases, "this is a cannon, a six-pounder, half buried in the creek. There must be other cannons scattered around. This would be a likely spot for a supply fort."

Anthony Wayne gave the painterman an admiring glance "You're getting better and better. After this unpleasent business is over —" he waved a hand at the woods in general, "— you can go back east and be a society painter!"

"Meanin' no disrespect, sir, I intend to go back to Columbia first and convince a certain young lady to be my wife."

The General curled his lip. "Bad business, marriage." He almost trembled with a sudden longing for the gay cafe-society days he had left in the sophisticated east. Gad! How he hated this swampy, buggy, snake-infested wilderness with all its discomforts! The gout in his foot throbbed painfully. "Well — a fort here, you say." With an effort he returned to the present. "Yes, it's a good idea to recover St. Clair's guns. The old boy may be good for something yet, eh, Alex?" he guffawed. "Ah, yes, I'll name it Recovery — Fort Recovery!"

"From there it's only around sixty miles to Grand Glaize and the heart of the Indian power!" Alex spoke rapidly, his eyes glowing. "Another fort here —" he pulled out another painting, "—at the point where the Maumee meets the Auglaize would break the power of the Crown."

"If Washington and Knox will allow me to break any power at all." A note of bitterness crept into Wayne's voice.

"Sir?"

"Exactly one year ago I wanted to build these roads and go after the Indians — but Washington refused. He and Knox said, 'We must not commit acts that could be construed as aggression of a weaker people!' " His face was dark purple. "You and I know that peace with the Indians is out of the question! They and their British father will continue to fight until the Ohio River is the boundary. If this happens, the British will build a chain of forts from the Upper Ohio to the Missisippi." He ran a hand over his face. "Shall peace be offered at so great a sacrifice of national honor and safety? Or shall our government demand the surrender of the lake margins?"

"Washington does not want to fight?"

Wayne frowned. "Washington and Knox are being pussy-footers about this whole business," he said. "Did you know that last summer Washington sent three men to Sandusky to give back the land ceded at Fort Harmar — except those granted to private companies — to evacuate both Fort Harmar and Fort Washington, and to make an outright gift of

$50,000 with $10,000 to be paid later, if the red man would let the Treaty of Harmar stand! Imagine! Americans — proud, free Americans — grovelling before savages!"

"What was the Indian reply?"

"I'm surprised you haven't heard all about it, living here among them."

"I don't discuss politics, sir, I just paint."

"Well the varmits said no, the monies were of no use to them. They advised giving it to the poor settlers to help them build new homes south of the Ohio River!"

"That was white of them," Alex could not help but laugh.

"Well, white or not, that ended negotiations! Washington could say the Americans had offered to be reasonable and the Indians had chosen not to be. So I received my orders to move into their country. I hope Washington does not change his bloody mind!"

Alex chuckled again at the Generals colorful choice of words. "You'll be president someday, sir," he volunteered.

"Not me, lad," barked Wayne. "I have no illusions as to my popularity. They say I'm a brute because I teach the Legions how to load their guns faster. Because I force them to dig breastworks and fight sham battles in the dead of winter. My men grow restless from boredom — my lieutenants plot against me. No, lad, old Tony Wayne will never be more than he is today. And may be less!" Then with a swift change of mood, he fingered the disk around his neck. "How do you like the American George Medallion?" he queried.

Alex studied the silver oval. One side pictured a bare-headed George Washington handing a peace pipe to an Indian; on the reverse side the Coat of Arms of the United States appeared beneath a cloudy sky through which the sun of victory broke. "I like it," he grinned. "I'll be mighty glad when I can wear one to show the world!"

"No one suspects you, do they?" Wayne asked anxiously.

"Well," Alex said ruefully, "I'm suspected of being a traitor and a british spy by a white captive living with the Indians' old prophetess, Cooh-coo-cheeh!"

"That's all to the good," Wayne assured him.

"Except that he's the brother of the girl I want to marry! Had to go and get himself captured!"

"But how did you know him before?"

"Came downriver with the family on their flatboat."

"Quite a coincidence," remarked the General.

"Quite," agreed Alex.

"Yes. Well, Alex, I'll be needing you at the new fort to lead us into Grand Glaize. Is there some way I could get the Legion into this town and take them by surprise?"

Alex pondered this for a moment. "It might be possible," he said slowly. "Give me a little time to work it out."

"Send me word by the usual messenger when you're ready."

"I was indeed surprised when he spoke of the George Medallion — almost ignored him."

"Seems he had a friend, an American boy captured somewhere in Virginia, who helped him and he's been loyal to us ever since."

He grasped Alex by his hand. "We've been here too long now, Alex. You must not risk being seen with me. If you are discovered it will mean a slow cruel death. They burned Crawford near here, I believe." The General limped painfully toward the woods. "My horse is hidden in here," he said. "Good luck, and farewell, my loyal friend. You have done well for your country."

Jubal watched as the two men parted, each going his own way. Then he crept miserably back to the house of Cooh-coo-cheeh. If he needed more proof of Alex's loyalty to the crown, here it was. With his own two eyes Jubal had seen him present the maps to a stranger wearing a silver medallion of the

King! Oh! If only he had been nearer and could have heard what they were saying! He was so quiet and subdued that Cooh-coo-cheeh was at first impressed.

"Cooh-coo-cheeh scold Sawendebans, turn him into good boy," she gloated. But when Jubal spent the remainder of the day moping before the fire, she began to worry. "I hurt you?" she inquired. "Cooh-coo-cheeh sing to Yellow Hair. Sawwat-tee sawwatty, Sawawkee meec hee noo kakoohonny! Kooquay nippee ta tsa. Waugh waw...." it was her favorite song, sung by a beaver to a dispairing hunter, telling him he will find game beyond the swollen stream. Jubal had always liked to hear her sing it, but today he did not smile.

"No 'twasn't you, Cooh-coo-cheeh," he answered. How could Alex be a turncoat? He thought of Polly, crying her eyes out at his capture. He clearly remembered the grizzled face of Increase Foster, a face that would never again give him a kindly smile. The only explanation he could think of for Alex's behavior was that his friend had switched loyalties after his capture to save his own skin. But to what lengths would a man go to save his own life? A slow fury burned inside the boy, and he burst out, "I hate him! I hate him!"

The winter days passed quitely. Soon the old year died and 1794 began. Sharp, frosty nights and days of warm sunshine began to replace the gray dullness of winter, and one morning Cooh-coo-cheeh announced it was sugar weather. She bustled around the cabin barking orders to Jubal and Quasay so rapidly that the two kept bumping into one another and finally gave up and collapsed on the floor, weak from giggling.

Packing one large brass kettle and several smaller ones, their bedding, a quantity of corn and beans and all their utensils except the hominy block, the old woman closed the cabin and placed a stick across the door. They crossed the Maumee below the mouth of the Auglaize and stopped at the lodge of Black Loon to pick up a horse and eat lunch. They packed all the baggage on the horse, said goodbye to Black Loon and his wife, and proceeded four or five miles down the river to beautiful open woods of sugar-maple trees interlaced with blue ash, elm and poplar. Here Cooh-coo-cheeh had for many years made her sugar, and here they found a comfortable bark shelter with everything necessary for making sugar. She kept Jubal and Quasay very busy dusting out and setting the troughs while she tapped the trees.

"Oogh!" she swung a stick at Jubal. "Sawendebans, cut logs then go catch fish for supper. Quasay, carry sap for old Grandmother!"

Jubal caught a six-pound catfish, which they cooked over hickory ashes until its white meat was flaky and tender. They had succotash and, for dessert, freshly-made maple sugar cakes. Then they carried more sap and cut more logs. Night after night they tended to the boiling water, and when they finally returned to the house on the hill they had enough sap to make one hundred pounds of sugar.

After the sugar-making, spring came swiftly. The scent of fragrant white-flowered apple trees and pink-blossomed ones filled the air with heady sweetness. The women and children worked in the fields planting kernels of corn in small mounds of moist earth. Jubal and Quasay, along with the other children from the town, planted squash and pumpkin in the sides of the mounds. But in spite of the glorious spring a heavy sense of danger hung over all the towns strung along the rivers. Jubal could see it reflected in Cooh-coo-cheeh as she moved about her daily tasks. She was silent and watchful. The town across the river was seething with milling, restless warriors. Farther downriver Blue Jacket's Town swarmed with strangers. War poles were being struck and the wampum was red, blood red. Many rumors came to the ears of those willing to listen. Rumors of the One Who Never Slept, who was bringing a vast army to destroy the Indian.

"He is like the Wind, who cannot be caught!"

"He is like a Tornado, who slashes the wilderness! He cannot be surprised — he knows all and sees all!"

One morning in June, Quasay came running up the hill shouting for her grandmother. "We are visited today by great chiefs," she cried, her black eyes flashing in her pretty face. "Blue Jacket comes, Buckongehelas comes — even Little Turtle! And many braves!"

Cooh-coo-cheeh, dressed in a yellow calico stroud, awaited her impressive visitors with dignity in the door of her cabin. They greeted each other politely, and she invited them inside to smoke a pipe of her own tobacco. Little Turtle, crafty war-chief of the Miamis, spoke first.

"We come to you, wise Ancient One, to learn of the future. You must speak to your spirits and inquire of them whether or not we shall be successful in finding the lost guns of St. Clair."

Arrogant, straight as a pine tree and almost as tall, Little Turtle stood before the old Priestess. His footlong earrings jangled as he tossed his head, and his three huge nose jewels glittered in the morning sunlight. "There is no time today for the pipe," he declared.

"Then you must leave me alone in my house," she ordered. "Quasay! Take our guests to the shed. You too, Sawendebans — out! Out!" She flailed her arms and slammed the door.

Quasay was a good hostess. She chatted politely with the chiefs and brought them corn bread to eat and cool fresh water to drink. Jubal sat and stared, fascinated by the richly dressed Indians. Cooh-coo-cheeh remained inside her cabin nearly an hour. During that time Jubal could hear noises which sounded like a stick striking the sides of the house and the brass kettles, silence, then a low humming sound.

"Her incantations," Quasay informed them.

Suddenly the door flew open and the princess burst forth, wild-eyed and disheveled. She raised both arms to the skies and gave a low moan. "It is bad!" she wailed. "No guns! No guns!" Tears streamed down her wrinkled old cheeks.

"What do you mean, Ancient One?" asked Blue Jacket. "What do the spirits say?"

The woman lowered her arms and sighed. "Spirits say — shadows and clouds which for two hundred years have gathered around the Indian now ready to close in the starless night of death."

And she would say no more.

Little Turtle turned to the others in the party. "You see," he murmured, "we must talk peace with the One Who Never Sleeps."

The others nodded assent.

Blue Jacket looked at them with contempt in his gray eyes. "Cowards! Turncoats!" he sneered. "Now is the time to save our lands for our children! Have we not twice defeated the Palefaces?"

"We have. But we have never fought such an enemy as the One Who Never Sleeps!" objected Little Turtle. "If we attack his new fort in search of St. Clair's guns, he will know our numbers, then never can we surprise him!"

Blue Jacket pondered this for a moment. "I agree — although if we could cut contact between his forts — we could drive him back to the Ohio River.

"It is too risky," counseled Buckongehelas. "This I know. But I doubt that I can keep my braves from attacking Fort Recovery."

"Nor I," added Blue Jacket. "My braves grow impatient."

"We must restrain them. We must save our strength for the final test." Little Turtle gave a signal and they made their farewells to Cooh-coo-cheeh, leaving her many presents.

A SPY IS CAUGHT

Heedless of their leader's orders, the impatient warriors screamed out of the forest on the morning of June thirtieth, throwing themselves against the stockaded walls of Fort Recovery. From the shores of Lake Erie came the Wyandot and Ottawa, from Lake Huron the Chippawa and from Lake Michigan the Pottawatie. In vain Little Turtle and Blue Jacket tried to call them back, but their recent victories were too heady for the warriors. To their dismay, the guns they sought were mounted in the American fortress, waiting to discharge a volley of death into the United Tribes. Discouraged, they fell back. And when at sunset the following evening the attack was over, they had gained some three hundred American horses and cattle and lost forever any chance they might have had to surprise Anthony Wayne.

"Where'd all the Injuns come from?" Jubal asked George Ironside one day when he and Quasay were buying flour for Cooh-coo-cheeh. The town was filled to overflowing with strange Indian and British fighters who milled around, drinking and talking. Inside the roomy warehouse of the British trader were gathered several braves, the two Girty brothers, Simon and James, and a friend of theirs named McKee.

"Oh, they come from New York, Pennslyvania, all around," replied the trader. "They're waiting for the Legion under old Mad Anthony Wayne."

"If we could only get the Legion together in one spot," worried McKee, "we could murder 'em! Jove! That attack on Recovery was a fool stunt."

"We defeated Harmar and St. Clair," James Girty reminded him. "We can beat this 'un — if he comes."

"He's coming," asserted George Ironside. "I can almost see the long shadow of Mad Anthony stretching across the territory!"

"I just missed seein' General Wayne twice," chirped Jubal. "Once in Columbia when he was on his way to Fort Washington, then again in Cincinnati. What's he like?"

"He's a wild man and a fine officer in battle," Simon Girty said. "I saw him once in Pennslyvania. He's a chunky man with reddish hair. They say he's been ill — and that it takes three men to lift him upon his horse. And we fear a man like that?" He gave an ugly laugh.

"He's good on his strategy," Ironside said. "Knew right where to build those wide roads of his — where to build those supply forts. The man's uncanny."

Simon Girty spat on the floor. "Uncanny my eye!" he snorted. "Wayne has more spies than a dog has fleas. And what his spies can't tell him he finds out by capturing lone Injuns and torturing them 'til they spill everything they know. Spies!"

"He has the best woodsmen on the frontier spying for him — Wells, the traitor! And Kibbey, and heaven knows how many other we don't know about!" added James.

"We'll find every one of 'em," vowed Simon, "and when we do —" he drew a finger across his throat. "You sneakin' Long Knives and your spies!" he leered at Jubal.

"You Tories have your spies too!" said Jubal hotly, remembering the painterman with a pang.

"What d'you know about our spies?" smirked Girty.

"More'n you think," snapped Jubal.

"Kid's just talkin', Simon," said George Ironside. "Pay him no heed."

Jubal hesitated. A small voice deep within him warned him to be quiet for once. But a more important, larger voice cried out that it would be a delight to reveal to these smug British that an American boy could discover their spies. "I ain't just talkin'!" He looked wise. "I've seen the painterman meetin' some man in the woods — and givin' him maps and talkin' to him!" he blurted out.

Simon Girty pulled slowly out of his slouch and exchanged a look with his brother. "You've what?" he bellowed.

"What man? Talking to what man in the woods?" cried McKee.

"Why, I don't know who he is." Jubal was taken back by their response. Some Tory wearin' a silver medallion and limping around. You ought to know who he is.'"

"Limping around?" Simon Girty murmured softly. "Limping around? _Limping?_"

"Talking to Alex — the painterman? Then those paintings of his were —" James Girty was silenced by a quick nod from his brother.

"Well, well, you are a sharp 'un aren't you?" Simon Girty patted Jubal on the shoulder. "I'll tell Alex to be more careful!" He winked at McKee and gave a shout of laughter.

Jubal was pretty impressed with himself. After all, it did no harm to let the British know they were not so smart as they thought! "Come on, Quasay," he swaggered. "Let's go home. I've got the flour."

Simon Girty waited until they were safely gone, then said, "That explains it all! The wide roads — the lost guns of Fort Recovery! Ah, well Mr. Alexander Keene, you shall pay dearly for this. Let's pay a visit to Blue Jacket, Jim. Comin' McKee?"

"Coming," said McKee grimly.

Jubal, blissfully unaware of what he had done, found a small black snake in the wet grass beside the river and chased Quasay all the way home, swinging it at her.

And so the uneasy summer passed. Quasay had refused to go to her own parents, prefering life with her grandmother. Cooh-coo-cheeh had many callers. They sat in front of her cabin in the dusk letting the cool breezes from the river sway their vermillion plumes. Jubal and Quasay sat nearby, listening to the news of the day.

"We have nothing to worry about," said the White Loon. "Wayne has left the main part of his army in Greenville. Surely we can win over a handful of men!"

"The British father has armed Fort Miamis, so they and the Long Knives must be at war."

"I have plenty of ammunition and equipment from the King's stores in Detroit," George Ironside informed the warriors.

"With the aid of the British father, we cannot fail." Blue Jacket was confident. He turned to Cooh-coo-cheeeh. "Are the spirits more favorable to their red children now, Ancient One?"

Cooh-coo-cheeh looked miserable. "It is the same with them.

As August approached, the valley sweltered in the grip of a sultry heat wave. The dry leaves withered and drifted earthward lifelessly and the rivers narrowed and seemed to stop flowing. Dust from many shuffling moccasined feet mingled with the heat haze and rose to give the sky the appearance of beaten brass. Blowing Snow acted as if each breath might be his last. He dug a deep hole in a shady spot and lay in it all day, panting. Then one day White Loon dashed into his mother's house with news.

"You must leave here at once," he cried. "A deserter from the army of the One Who Never Sleeps came! The Americans are almost here — they will kill and burn any Indian they find! Take plenty of food!"

"Can I stay?" asked Jubal. "They won't kill me — I'm no Injun." It might be his only chance to get home again, he thought.

"No! No! No!" Cooh-coo-cheeh was in a terrible temper. "You come with us!" Never would she admit how fond she had become of this yellow-haired boy. And what a fine husband he would make for Quasay.

She gathered as many of her utensils as she could carry, packing the kettles with dried squash and beans and jerked venison, and they joined the little army of women and children marching slowly upriver. Past the rapids of the Maumee, beneath the guns of the Fort Miamis they shuffled in the blistering heat. About three miles from the bristling guns of the British fort they stopped, and prepared to wait until the Paleface Army was driven out. Here they would be safe: the crown would see to that. The old Prophetess and her family were given a comfortable bark cabin by themselves.

Quasay was in her usual high spirits, teasing Blowing Snow with a switch and kicking through dry leaves that covered the ground. Cooh-coo-cheeh was inconsolable. That her spirits had spoken true she was sure. "It is the end of the red man," she crooned softly over and over again. "We follow the path into the starless night of death. Think kindly of Cooh-coo-cheeh, Sawendebans!"

Runners from the United Tribes kept them imformed of daily happenings. On the morning of August eighth a runner came and announced with pride that the Americans had arrived in Grand Glaize and were astounded to find the town deserted and all provisions gone. "Already we have outsmarted the Paleface One!"

Jubal lay awake a long time that night. The heat was smothering. And he was worried. If the Indians won a third victory, he feared for his family in Columbia. For this time the white man would be driven south of the Ohio River — or murdered. Oh! If there were only something he could do! He tossed and turned, finally deciding to go outside to catch whatever breeze there might be.

The little makeshift village was quiet and dark. But far off in the forest he caught a glimpse of a fire torch. Then another and another, until a string of them wound through the starless night toward their town. He slipped into the hut and wakened Quasay. "What is it, Quasay?" he queried pointing to the bright parade.

"I not know," replied the girl. "Wait Sawendebans, listen for the yell, then we know."

They sat in comfortable silence watching the torches draw closer. Then a terrible, high pitched scream bent the stillness of the night.

"Ah, it is the halloo of a captured prisoner. A very important prisoner," she told Jubal. "Maybe the One Who Never Sleeps himself!"

At the first halloo the village sprang to life. People gathered around the campfire to await the captive, talking excitedly. Hand in hand Quasay and Jubal ran to join the restless throng. They had not long to wait before a small band of Indians marching single file entered the village with a prisoner in their midst. The captive was bound hand and foot and looked weary, but his head was held high and his eyes were flashing. Jubal caught his breath as he recognized his old friend, the painterman!

Simon Girty was beside Alex holding on to a leather thong attached to the painterman's ankle. The renegade seemed to be looking for someone in the crowd — and stopped looking when he saw Jubal. "Come here, Yellow Hair!" he called. "I've a present for you!"

Jubal shot a stricken look toward Alex and made his way through the crowd of Indians to meet the renegade. Simon Girty, his face twisted in an amused grimace, removed a silver King George Medallion from around his neck and placed it over Jubal's head.

"The British father will be pleased with you, small Long Knife," he mocked. "You have helped us capture one of Wayne's most valuable spies!"

THE FAT INDIAN

Jubal thought his heart would stop beating.

"W — Wayne's spy?" he gasped. "But I — I thought —" the ground seemed to fall out from under him. "How did I help you?"

"That day in Ironside's Store when you said you had seen Alex give his paintings to a man who limped! Tony Wayne has gout in his foot so bad he limps worse every day." Simon Girty laughed. "So you see, lad, you're more loyal to the crown than you know!"

"But —"

"Blue Jacket always said his paintings were maps — but no one believed him until then," Girty continued. "You put the finger on him, Sawendebans!"

Desperately Jubal turned to Alex. "But the man I saw you with wore a silver medallion — just like this one!" he cried.

"Not exactly, Jube," replied the painterman in a tired voice. "It was a George Medallion all right, but the George was George Washington."

"Oh! Oh!" Jubal moaned. "Oh Alex, I didn't know! I never thought you might be on our side! I thought you were a British agent and I hated you for it!"

"You only believed what you saw," Alex told him. "Don't worry, Jube, I won't tell them a thing. One thing, Jubal. If....if I don't get out of this, tell Polly I...I loved her and sure wanted her for my wife."

Their conversation was ended abruptly as two Indians jerked Alex away. A white-tipped brush fell from the pack he carried. Jubal turned away to hide the hot tears that sprang to his eyes as he remembered that carefree day on the Youghiogheny when he and Alex had cut Thankful's tail-tip. Angry, Jubal ripped off Girty's medallion tossed it to the ground and, like a wounded animal crept back to the bark hut. Cooh-coocheeh was awake, but had remained inside.

"What will they do to him, Cooh-coo-cheeh?" whispered Jubal.

"He will die," answered the old woman. "He will be tied to the post for days and days and slowly tortured until he begs for a bullet to end his suffering —"

"Stop it!" cried the boy. "Can't you do something?" He was sick with horror and guilt. It was all his fault! If only he had kept still that day in George Ironside's store. If only he had not felt the need to impress the Girtys with how smart he, Jubal Hewitt, loyal American, was! For it was as plain as the nose on his face now. Jubal Hewitt was a stupid, braggy boy who liked to talk too much. How well the seeds Em Foster had sewed so many months ago had grown to release their poison, for it was she who had first suggested the painterman was in the pay of the Crown. But try as he would, he could blame no one but himself. "Ohhh!" He gave a strangled cry of despair and spent the rest of the night dreaming terrible dreams of people burning at the stake.

Early the next morning Jubal left the hut. Sure enough, there was Alex, pale and drawn, bound to a stake in the ground. All alone the painterman faced a prolonged death, singing "The Blue Bells of Scotland" in a cheerful, off-key voice.

"Alex! Alex!" Jubal started to run to his friend, but was halted by the fat Indian they called Round-as-a-Pumpkin.

"You cannot talk to him," said the Indian. "There is ugliness in the hearts of the braves today. They swear they will burn anyone who talks to the painterman. Go away!"

"Do as he says, Jube," called out the prisoner sharply.

Jubal stared at him a moment, then with a hoarse cry turned and ran blindly into the scraggly underbrush that edged the river. He threw himself over a log and gazed into the shallow amber water. A school of tiny minnows darted by. A curious crawdad peered out of its hole in the mud, then went on about its business. Maybe he could think of some way to set Alex free at night. Quasay, he was sure, would help. She liked Alex. Cooh-coo-cheeh might aid them. Alex had built her a fine shed for the Green corn Dance. Perhaps she could call upon her spirit friends. They seemed obliging.

A fish leapt out of the water and plopped back with a long splash making Jubal jump. It splashed again — and then again! Funny, he thought, he could see the splash but not the fish. It looked like someone throwing stones. Then something sharp struck his forehead, and he scrambled up and looked around. Someone was throwing pebbles to attract his attention. But who? And from where? A slight movement in a clump of bushes a few yards away caught his eye and he walked over and pulled apart the branches. There, hidden in a small dip, crouched Round-as-a-Pumpkin. Placing a forefinger across his mouth he motioned for Jubal to sit beside him.

"No one saw you come here?" he asked.

"They're all back in the village thinkin' up ways to kill Alex," replied Jubal bitterly.

"It is your fault he is where he is."

Jubal swallowed. "I know," he mumbled.

"Would you like to help him and make up for what you have done?"

"Oh! I would! But how? Will it save his life?"

"It might. It might not. But it will save your people."

Jubal hesitated. If it would not save the friend he had wronged so terribly, what was the use? His accomplice read his thoughts. "Is it not better one should die for many? Your family, perhaps, or friends? You have a brother?"

"A sister."

"Maybe you would like to her see her head on the end of a pike?"

Jubal shivered at the thought of Polly's pretty chestnut curls. "What can I do?" he asked hastily. "And how do I know you're not trickin' me?"

"You don't, you must have faith."

He was right. Jubal was at the end of his rope. "What can I do?" he murmured.

"Wayne and his Legion are at Grand Glaize. They build a big fort there, then move on to another supply fort they call Fort Deposit. Go there, speak to no one but General Wayne. Tell him you speak for the George Medallion, which has been captured and cannot speak for itself. Tell him the Indians will expect an attack on the seventeenth. Can you remember that? The seventeenth. It is very important."

"But I don't understand."

"It is better you do not. Then if you are captured, you cannot talk about it."

Jubal flushed. "I ain't gonna talk — ever again! Even if they would torture me!"

"Some talk without torture."

"I know. What about Alex? Will they...will they —"

"That is why I send the message with you instead of going myself. I think I can persuade them to keep him until after the battle. I shall try."

"And if they won't?"

The man shrugged. "It is part of his job. Go, Yellow Hair, and speak to no one of this. It is very important that

Wayne gets this message today. Luck." He gave the boy a gentle shove toward the beach. "Follow the river then cut across the field of the Fallen Timbers. There, beyond a great plain, you will find the one you seek."

Jubal picked his way through prickly blackberry bushes and thorny brambles that tore at his flesh. Swarms of mosquitoes rose from their nests near the river to feed on him, and perspiration matted his blond hair close to his head. He met no one. He walked toe first as he had seen the warriors in Grand Glaize track their prey. Silently he slipped from tree to tree, always keeping a sharp lookout. He was proud of himself, for even the excitable squirrels scarcely noticed his passing. Suddenly he was startled by a soft "thump," accompanied by a great deal of thrashing and rustling. Swiftly he crouched behind a tree trunk and peeked around.

It was Quasay, sprawled on her stomach on the mossy ground. Around her ankle was the wild grape vine that tripped her. Eyes shut tight, she was shaking with muffled laughter.

"Quasay! What are you doing here? Why are you following me?" cried Jubal in panic.

"Watching you be big Indian brave," giggled the girl. "Very quiet, on big mission. Oh, very funny!"

"Quasay — " Had she heard? A sharp pang clutched Jubal. Was he never to do anything right? If the painterman died it would be on his conscience forever. "How long have you been following me?"

Quasay gave him an arch look. "You not hear Quasay?" she asked.

"No."

"Quasay go with Sawendebans?"

"No!"

"Then Quasay tell Cooh-coo-cheeh that you run away!"

"Shucks!" He had no choice. "All right, come on, then," he said grudgingly.

"Quasay knows shortcut." She held out a little brown hand. "Come, Yellow Hair, follow!"

Jubal's mouth dropped open. "You heard everything?"

She nodded.

"But — "

"Painterman always good to Quasay and to Cooh-coo-cheeh. We not want to see him tortured," she shuddered.

"But — you're an Injun — "

"Indians not kill for pleasure of killing, Sawendebans," retorted Quasay. "Indian say, 'An eye for an eye and a tooth for a tooth and blood for blood!' Don't be so dumb, Paleface!"

Jubal felt very small. Taking Quasay's hand, he followed in silence. He liked this bright-eyed, fun-loving Indian girl better than any girl he had ever known except Polly. She led him along a narrow path that skirted a deep woods on one side and fell off into a steep ravine on the other. Farther along the trail the woods gave way to a clearing crisscrossed with decaying fallen timber.

"Great wind come, many moons ago, blow trees over," Quasay told him as they struggled over the huge rotten logs.

At the end of the woods they found a plain of tall grass. Here Quasay stopped, and pointing to a small log building in the distance, said, "Fort Deposit."

"Well, come on," Jubal pulled her along with him.

"No. I go back to Cooh-coo-cheeh." Quasay held back, and to Jubal's surprise there were tears glistening in the black eyes of the Indian girl.

"Quasay, what's wrong?"

"We never meet again, Sawendebans," she said simply. "Goodbye."

"Quasay!" Jubal stared at her. "We'll meet again! I'm coming back tonight to stay 'til I'm ransomed. Besides, I couldn't leave Alex there alone!"

A bright tear rolled down Quasay's cheek. "No. Cooh-coo-cheeh has spoken to the spirits of the dead. Big battle comes

— then Indian moves west into land where sun sets."

Jubal brushed the tear away from her face and swallowed shyly. Funny, he had never before felt shy with Quasay. She had been like a pesty little sister until now. But now he saw that she was a young lady, and a pretty one, too. "But Quasay, I'm to marry you. Cooh-coo-cheeh said so!" He tried a grin.

She took his hand and pressed it briefly to her cheek, then with a flash of white teeth in her brown little face, she turned and ran as fast as she could through the fallen timber. Jubal watched until her flying figure disappeared into the woods, then started off for the fort. In spite of the spirits, he would see Quasay tonight!

THE BATTLE!

A sentry stopped him at the entrance of the supply fort. "Here, you, where d'ya think yer goin'?" he demanded.

"I must see General Wayne," said Jubal.

"Well now," the sentry grinned, "and who shall I tell him's callin'?"

Jubal scowled. The guard walked all around the boy, looking him over from head to foot. "I'll be danged! A yallar haired Injun callin' on the Gen'ral."

"I ain't no Injun!" said Jubal. "I was captured 'bout a year ago. I have a message for the General."

"Now, boy, the Gen'ral's a pretty busy man. You run along back where you came from and don't pester."

Jubal snorted in exasperation. "Please, sir, it's very important!"

It was the "sir" that did it. Straightening his shoulders, the sentry placed his rifle snout against Jubal's back and marched the boy to a tent in the center of the stockade. "You win, sonny," he laughed. "Gen'ral Wayne, sir, here's someone ta see you. A yaller haired Injun boy! Ho ho!"

"Bring him in, sentry," a voice ordered.

Anthony Wayne had three aides with him, and hovering on the sidelines was old Solomon. "Well, well," the General looked up from his maps — Alex's maps, Jubal noticed. "Have our English adversaries come to drafting beardless youths?" he chuckled.

Jubal studied the man in front of him. Sure enough, it was the same stocky man he had seen with Alex in the oak woods. Except this man looked ill. His arms and legs were wrapped in flannel bandages and his eyes were dull with pain. On his breast lay the silver medallion. And now, now that it was too late, Jubal could see the figures in relief on the disk: one an Indian, the other a likeness of George Washington. Oh, he thought, if only he had been able to see it that day in the woods — or better still, if he had seen Anthony Wayne in Columbia, or in Cincinnati. If...if! His good friend would not now be tied to a stake in the blistering heat.

"I have a message for you, sir," Jubal said.

"Pay no attention to him, sir," said one of the aides. "He's undoubtedly a child of one of the English traders at Grand Glaize and loyal to the Crown. It's a dirty Tory trick!"

Jubal's temper flared. "That's not true!" he shouted. "I'm Jubal Hewitt from the Columbia settlement — and Solomon, if you don't remember me, then I'll freshen your memory!" He took a flying leap at Solomon's knees, bringing him down as he had over a year before.

The old man sighed deeply from his awkward position on the tent floor. "It's him, sir," he said. "He speaks the truth. Same yellow hair. I'd know the brat anywhere!"

Wayne stood up slowly and painfully. "Who sent you, boy?"

"The fat Injun, Round-as-a-Pumpkin. He said, 'Tell Wayne the silver George Medallion has been captured and cannot speak!' He said, 'Tell him the Injuns will expect an attack on the seventeenth!' That's what he said, sir. On the seventeenth! Oh, sir, it was all my fault. I thought Alex was a British spy and I saw — "

"Later, boy, later!" Wayne raised a hand for silence. "On the seventeenth, eh? Good! Good. Men," he said turning to his aides, "we shall attack on the twentieth — if attack is necessary.

"The twentieth, sir? But the boy said — "

"That's just it. The Indians have a belief that if a man is shot in the body when he is empty, there is not half so much danger of the ball passing through the bowels as when they are full. So they fast before a battle — if they know when that battle is to be." He laughed. "They expect an attack on the seventeenth, so no food all that day. They'll think surely the eighteenth. No food that day — and by the twentieth those who have not left seeking nourishment will be too weak to put up much resistance."

"But if the Canadian Militia and the Force of British Regulars stationed at Fort Miamis decide to fight — what then?"

"That would mean war with the Crown again, and the British don't want that, believe me," replied Wayne crisply. Turning to Jubal, he said, "Don't worry about your painterman friend. We'll get him back. And you, boy, are pretty much of a hero yourself, eh, Solomon?"

The old man gave a grudging nod, muttering about what a small world it was getting to be.

"Fix a bunk for the boy," Wayne ordered. "You'd better stay here until this is settled one way or the other."

"But sir, I'd like to go back. Just to say goodbye."

"You can say goodbye later. It wouldn't be safe for you to return now — someone may have seen you come here." Wayne patted Jubal on the back and hobbled out of the tent.

The eighteenth passed slowly for Jubal. The men were all kind to him and showed him where they guessed the battle would take place. "Lookit them peaceful woods," one grizzled veteran of the Revolution pointed out. "Ye'd never think they was a thousand red skins hidin' there."

Once Mad Anthony limped up to the boy, carrying one of Alex's paintings under his arm. "Thanks to your 'British spy' friend, we stand here between the Indian army at the headwaters and the British at Fort Miamis, ready to crush either objective with equal might. We have a line of supply forts stretching from here to the Ohio River, and now we'll soon know whether this war will be between us and the Indians, or whether it will be war for freedom with the Crown."

"But yesterday you said the Crown does not want another war," Jubal objected.

"I said that to my aides. I'm not so sure myself." Wayne winked at Jubal.

"I'd sure like to help Alex somehow," moped Jubal.

"Don't worry, lad, he's tough."

The nineteenth seemed to last an eternity. The weather was brooding, and when the high fog broke up in the late afternoon it revealed towering masses of white thunderheads.

Showers in the early morning of the twentieth wakened Jubal. He could feel a tense undercurrent of excitement running through the supply fort this morning. He heard an aide named Harrison say to General Wayne, "Give us your orders now, sir! You'll get into the thick of battle and forget the necessary field orders."

"That's right, sir!" chimed in Campbell, a dragoon leader.

Anthony Wayne chuckled. "If I do, Lieutenant Harrison, recollect the standing order of the day is, 'Charge the rascals with the bayonets!'"

Jubal did not dally in bed another second. Tossing aside his thin coverlet, he dashed out in time to see three men hoist the General into his saddle. A soldier left with a flag of truce to the United Tribes, and Wayne started without waiting for a reply. As they marched along the narrow trail the Legion was on the right, flanked by the Maumee. A brigade of mounted volunteers rode on the left and another in the rear. A select battalion of Kentucky mounted volunteers led the Legion, directed by Wayne to keep well in advance so as to give time for the troops to form in case of ambush. Jubal, standing beside old Solomon, watched the magnificent spectacle of American strength and thought his heart would burst with pride. "Ain't they grand?" he whispered.

"Aye, lad, that they are!" answered Solomon. "Come along, let's follow 'em!"

Both were under the strictest orders to remain at Fort Deposit and neither had the slightest intention of obeying. They waited until the head of the last mounted soldier disappeared across the plain, then both started off at a trot. On and on they went, and still nothing but the clip-clop of horse hooves and the clanking of swords broke the morning stillness. "Maybe they ain't gonna fight, Solomon," said Jubal, a worried frown puckering his brows. "We'll have to do something about Alex pretty soon. He can't last much longer in this heat — even if the Injuns don't kill him."

The advance corps had gone about five miles when the whole world seemed to explode. Hundreds of rifles cracked, and writhing spirals of white smoke rose from the field of fallen timbers. The Kentucky volunteers staggered before the volley of death from the Indian guns.

Wild-eyed horses reared, mortally wounded men sliding from their backs. Survivors swung about, spurred their horses, and, to Jubal's dismay, galloped back to safety. This quick dash threw the regulars into confusion and they too broke and ran. The whole van of the Legion crumpled and gave way. Wayne, his face purple, forgot the pain, jabbed his spurs into his stallion's flanks and charged forward, swearing at the top of his lungs.

"Clear the enemy from the tall grass," he screamed to Campbell as the volunteers on the right, fearing ambush, hesitated to advance. "The rascals are stronger in front! Scott, take your Kentuckians and get them from behind!"

"They're streched in three straight lines from the river," shouted Campbell.

"Go in there and flush 'em out," screamed Wayne, half standing in his stirrups. "Deliver your bullets close and well in order to fire on their backs — then they'll have no time to reload!"

Campbell's men rallied and galloped forward, their broadswords swinging in the air, their horses jumping over fallen timber, ramming their way pell-mell into the ambush.

Little Turtle's sharpshooters let burst with a second volley. Campbell fell dead. Again his men wavered. The Indians, thinking their work was done, jumped from their hiding places and ran into the woods on the left.

Jubal clutched Solomon's bony arm. "They're winnin'!" he cried. "Oh, Solomon, they're murderin' the General!"

"It's not over yet," said Solomon gruffly.

Once again the furious figure of Mad Anthony Wayne loomed up in the cloud of smoke. Jubal saw him tear the flannel bandages from his arms and gallop from flank to flank, shouting, "Hamtrack, charge! Wilkinen, drive ahead! Go — you're in the center, use your bayonets! What d'ye think you have 'em for? To pick your teeth? Charge the bloody —" the rest of his angry words were drowned out by the screams of the Indians and the triumphant yells of the Legion as the enemy began to give ground.

Great clouds of dust rose from the battle ground. The British guns remained silent. In the confusion Jubal caught a glimpse of a negro from Kentucky firing three shots at three Indians trying to swim the river. Three times his bullets found their marks, and he turned to give Jubal and Solomon a brilliant flash of white teeth before tearing on to find more Indians and British to kill. Here and there red men and white were locked in hand to hand combat. Above the yelling and the din of battle, Jubal heard Solomon shouting to him. "The

Legion's driven them back! Come on lad, let's get back to the fort. If Wayne should see us here in the temper he's in, he'd have us both shot for disobedience!"

They ran back to the temporary Fort Deposit, where the reserve men were cheering and slapping each other on the back in wild excitement. The battle of Fallen Timbers had lasted exactly forty minutes!

The sun, a huge orange ball, set that evening through a haze of stale rifle smoke and dust, but no one at Deposit noticed. Messengers returned from the front reciting tales of bravery and triumph, and of the defeat of the Indian.

"You should've seen the Injuns run! Scared to death they was! Threw down their guns and ran to Fort Miamis for help and shelter. Blue Jacket and Little Turtle and that young Shawnee Tecumseh all poundin' on the gates and the British locked the doors agin' 'em!"

Another soldier told of General Wayne's bold action. "Wayne drew the whole Legion up in front of Fort Miamis and rode within pistol shot of the works, openly challenging its defenses. Then the British Commandant yelled out that he knew of no war between Great Britian and America — and Wayne said he'd like to answer that 'un from the muzzles of his small arms!"

"It worked like the Gen'ral said! Half the Injuns had gone to their towns for food!"

Jubal hung around the entrance of the fort. Surely the General would not forget Alex! Soon after dark his wait was rewarded, as two soldiers came out of the night, supporting a sagging figure between them.

"Alex! Alex!" Jubal's heart pounded hard. "Oh, he's not dead, is he?"

"Not quite, lad," answered one of the soldiers. "Though why he's not I don't know!"

Alex's head lolled on his shoulder. He was only semiconscious.

"I don't either," said the other soldier, rubbing the side of his head. "Those squaws were meaner 'n any brave I ever met! They sure wanted to keep this 'un!"

"Mostly he's hungry and tired," said the first "He's not as bad off as I expected. Someone must have given him a little food and water — else he'd be dead by now."

And I know who, thought Jubal gratefully. Oh, Quasay, thank you! And Cooh-coo-cheeh, yes, and the fat Injun, Round-as-a-Pumpkin. Thank you all! You kept me from being a murderer!

A week later, having wearied of taunting the British at Fort Miamis, Anthony Wayne returned with his army to Fort Defiance. Alex, much thinner for his experience but well on the mend, walked with Jubal and old Solomon.

"What will happen to Cooh-coo-cheeh and Quasay and the others?" asked Jubal.

"They will stay where they are for the time being," answered Alex. "Then sooner or later they will go west."

"Just like Cooh-coo-cheeh's spirits said," murmured Jubal.

Just then Anthony Wayne galloped up. "Ho there, Alex," he shouted. "Before I forget — I'll want you with me in Greenville to help round up the chiefs for the peace treaties!"

Alex looked unhappy. "Sir, if I may — I'd like a short leave."

"What for?" roared Wayne.

"To get married".

"Oh." Mad Anthony grinned. "Bad business," he reminded the painterman.

"And to take this yellow-haired Injun back to his family. He'll be m' little brother soon — I hope!"

"Hope he doesn't get any more crackpot ideas about you," Wayne chuckled.

"Sir, I'd never live through another one!" breathed Alex. "With your leave, sir, we'll spend a day or so at Defiance, then start for home. How's that sound, Jube?"

Home.

"Home." Jubal whispered the word. "Home." He savored the sound. "Oh! HOME!"

The scalp-yell he gave was the most authentic of his scalp-yelling career.